SWARM

OPERATION STING

STRIPES PUBLISHING
An imprint of Little Tiger Press
1 The Coda Centre, 189 Munster Road,
London SW6 6AW

A paperback original
First published in Great Britain in 2014

ISBN: 978-1-84715-437-8

A CIP catalogue record for this book is available
from the British Library.

Printed and bound in the UK.

10 9 8 7 6 5 4 3 2 1

SIMON CHESHIRE

Stripes

DEPARTMENT OF MICRO-ROBOTIC INTELLIGENCE

SPECIALISTS IN NANOTECHNOLOGY AND BIOMIMICRY

HEAD OF DEPARTMENT

Beatrice Maynard: Code name QUEEN BEE

HUMAN OPERATIVES

Prof. Thomas Miller: TECHNICIAN
Alfred Berners: PROGRAMMER
Simon Turing: DATA ANALYST

SWARM OPERATIVES

WIDOW

DIVISION: Spider
LENGTH: 1.5 cm
WEIGHT: 1 gram
FEATURES:
- 360° vision and recording function
- Produces silk threads and webs stronger than steel
- Extremely venomous bite
- Can walk on any surface – horizontal, vertical or upside down

CHOPPER

DIVISION: Dragonfly
LENGTH: 12 cm
WEIGHT: 0.8 grams
FEATURES:
- Telescopic vision with zoom, scanning and recording functions
- Night vision and thermal imaging abilities
- High-speed flight with super control and rapid directional change

NERO

DIVISION: Scorpion
LENGTH: 12 cm
WEIGHT: 30 grams
FEATURES:
- Strong, impact-resistant exoskeleton
- Pincers to grab and hold, with high dexterity
- Venomous sting in tail
- Capable of high-speed attack movements

SABRE

DIVISION: Mosquito
LENGTH: 2 cm
WEIGHT: 2.5 milligrams
FEATURES:
- Long proboscis (mouthparts) for extracting DNA and injecting tracking technology and liquids to cause paralysis or memory loss
- Specialist in stealth movement without detection
- Capable of recording low frequency, low-volume sound

HERCULES

DIVISION: Stag beetle
LENGTH: 5 cm
WEIGHT: 50 grams
FEATURES:
- Extra-tough membrane on wing shells to withstand extreme force and pressure
- Serrated claw for sawing through any material
- Can lay surveillance 'eggs' for tracking and data analysis

MORPH

DIVISION: Centipede
LENGTH: 5 cm (10 cm when fully extended)
WEIGHT: 100 milligrams
FEATURES:
- Flexible, gelatinous body with super-strong grip
- Ability to dig and burrow
- Laser-mapping sensory functions

SIRENA

DIVISION: Butterfly
LENGTH: 7 cm
WEIGHT: 0.3 grams
FEATURES:
- Uses beauty rather than stealth for protection
- Expert in reconnaissance missions – can gather environmental data through high-sensitivity antennae

CHAPTER ONE

"Queen Bee to agents! Prepare to move out!"

Two electronic voices replied, one after the other. "I'm live, Queen Bee."

Queen Bee sat in a high-backed black leather chair, in front of a wide bank of brightly lit screens and readouts. She was a tall woman with a shock of blonde hair and a smartly cut suit. She wore a pair of glasses with small, circular lenses that reflected the rapidly shifting light from the screens. Behind the lenses, her steely grey eyes darted from one readout to another, soaking up information. Her age was difficult to work out from her looks, but her slightly pursed lips, and the way her long fingers tapped slowly on the arms of her chair, showed that she meant business.

One of the screens in front of her showed a man coming out of an office block. Numbers and graphs danced across the lower part of the image, sensor readings of everything from the air temperature at his location to his current heart rate.

Queen Bee leaned forward and spoke into a microphone, which jutted out on a long, flexible stalk. "Chopper, begin data recording."

"Logged, Queen Bee," said one of the electronic voices. It had a slightly lower tone than the other one.

Outside the office block, Marcus Oliphant sniffed at the morning breeze for a moment. He was a tall, stringy man with bushy eyebrows and a loping walk. His nose wrinkled. The smell of vehicle exhaust seemed stronger than usual today. He took a tighter grip of the small metal case he was carrying, then set off along the street. The traffic of central London rumbled and roared past.

A long set of black-painted railings ran alongside him. He didn't notice two insects perched on top. One was a tiny mosquito, the other a large, iridescent dragonfly. At least, that's what they appeared to be. They didn't jump and flit like insects usually do. Instead, they seemed to be watching him.

As he walked off down the road, the insects' wings buzzed into life, and they rose into the air, following him at a short distance.

As the insects rose, so the image on the screen in front of Queen Bee shifted and moved.

Queen Bee swung around in her chair. Sitting behind her were half a dozen people with serious, quizzical expressions on their faces. Among them were the Home Secretary, the head of MI5 and Queen Bee's boss, the leader of the UK's Secret Intelligence Agency.

"As you can see, ladies and gentlemen," said

Queen Bee, "the subject has no idea that he's being tailed. Our micro-robots are much more effective than normal secret service agents, with their blindingly obvious dark glasses and their suspiciously unmarked fast cars."

The head of MI5 shuffled grumpily in his seat. "And much more expensive. How much are these technological toy soldiers costing, Home Secretary? You gave the SIA the go-ahead for this programme."

The Home Secretary looked slightly uncomfortable. "A lot. I'm afraid I don't have the figures to hand," she muttered.

"The latest technology is never cheap," said Queen Bee. "But my section, the Department of Micro-robotic Intelligence, has capabilities that make it priceless. The existence of SWARM is known only to my staff, and to the people in this room. However, nanotechnology is the future. Micro-robots will soon dominate the worlds of spying and crime investigation. These SWARM operatives are the most advanced robots on Earth. On the outside, they are almost indistinguishable from real insects, yet each has equipment and capabilities that make the average undercover agent look like a caveman."

The Home Secretary pointed to the screen. "Who is that man? What's this demonstration supposed to prove?"

"He's Marcus Oliphant, leader of the team that's developed the new Whiplash weapon," said Queen Bee. "It has been created by a private company, Techna-Stik International, and is being sold to the British government. The prototype is in that metal case there – it's only the size of a matchbox. He's on his way to meet with your own officials, Home Secretary, and show them the progress that's been made. I've asked for my robots to shadow him today, to show their effectiveness. Normally, an MI5 operative would be assigned, but since Whiplash is every bit as secret as SWARM, this man's visit has been judged low risk. No unauthorized person could possibly know what he's carrying."

"Whiplash?" said the Home Secretary. "Have I been briefed on that?" She turned to the man beside her.

"It's an EMP device," said the head of MI5.

"Extremely dangerous in the wrong hands."

"Extremely dangerous even in the right hands," muttered Queen Bee.

"EMP?" frowned the Home Secretary.

"Electro-magnetic pulse," explained Queen Bee. "It emits an invisible wave of energy which knocks out all electrical circuits. Fries them beyond repair. It does almost no physical damage, but destroys electronics – everything from air-traffic control to TV remotes. Vehicles, computers, the lot, all made useless."

"Whiplash shoots a narrow EMP beam across a few kilometres," said the head of MI5. "It's designed to target and disable enemy systems."

Suddenly, the high electronic voice of the mosquito cut across the air. "Sabre to Queen Bee. Suspicious activity detected."

Queen Bee leaned forward and spoke into the microphone. "Specify."

Out on the street, Chopper the robotic dragonfly whipped around in mid-air to direct his high-definition cameras towards a vehicle approaching from behind. His eyes zoomed in to reveal a powerful, dark blue BMW that was slowing down, causing cars behind it to overtake.

Chopper transmitted the data back to Queen Bee at SWARM headquarters. "The registration number does not match the car type listed on the national database," he said. "Stolen car, I think. Or stolen licence plates."

"Can you get a look at the driver?" radioed Queen Bee.

Chopper adjusted the thermal imaging in his eyes. "Negative, Queen Bee, too many reflections off the glass."

"Sabre," said Queen Bee, "stay close to the target."

"Logged," replied the mosquito. He buzzed closer to Oliphant, the man with the metal case, who took a casual swat at his shoulder.

Suddenly, the BMW roared ahead. Swerving violently, it bounced up on to the pavement in front of Oliphant, its brakes squealing. The doors were flung open and four men wearing balaclavas jumped out.

Oliphant stood open-mouthed, too alarmed to run. The man who'd been driving grabbed the metal case and knocked Oliphant flying with a sharp punch.

"Attack mode," said Chopper calmly. "Target compromised."

A tiny, needle-like proboscis flicked forward from Sabre's head. He dived swiftly towards the driver and stabbed at the man's neck in a lightning movement.

"Oww!" yelled the driver. "What was—?" Then he twitched, wide-eyed, dropped the metal case and toppled forward on to the pavement.

"Freezer sting delivered," said Sabre.

The other three men hauled the driver to his feet, grabbed the case and quickly got back into the BMW. Chopper circled, recording every detail of the attackers and their car. Oliphant sat on the pavement, dazed and rubbing his jaw.

The car lurched into life, roared around in a U-turn and sprang back on to the road. An approaching bus braked hard to avoid a collision and blasted its horn at the BMW. A small group of pedestrians were gathering around Oliphant, offering help. One was already calling the police on his mobile.

"The human is receiving assistance," said Chopper. "Pursue the weapon."

Chopper and Sabre swung round and darted off down the street after the BMW.

Queen Bee's voice buzzed in the insects' receivers. "Get to that car! Sabre, inject a tracker into one of those men!"

"Logged," said Sabre.

Chopper's vision zoomed in on the car as it raced ahead. "Windows closed. No entry. We may be able to gain access through an air vent."

Both insect robots flew at maximum speed. Chopper the dragonfly was larger and faster through the air than Sabre the mosquito, but even he struggled to keep up with the BMW. The car was weaving through the traffic, honking other vehicles out of the way and shifting up a gear.

"Personal speed limits reached," said Chopper. "The car's too fast for us. We will lose it in 19.4 seconds."

"Suggestion," piped up Sabre. "I can inject a

micro-explosive into one of the car's tyres. That will force it to stop."

Chopper paused, his miniature circuits making complex calculations. "Chance of success on a moving vehicle is only nine per cent. That action is not advised."

Sabre computed the information. "Your advice is ignored. I'm going to attempt it. The mission comes first. Our orders were to safeguard Whiplash, so now we must recover it."

The BMW sped on, shooting through a red light and turning left into a smaller road lined with parked cars.

Sabre angled his wings for a sharp descent, and swooped low alongside the car. He could feel the mechanisms inside his robot body overloading. He wasn't designed to move at this kind of speed!

He flew lower still, level with the car's wheels. The roar of the BMW's engine was deafening. The sound reverberated off the road and the parked cars.

Sabre's computer brain concentrated on flying steady. If he swung just a few centimetres to either side, he'd end up a smear on the tarmac.

Inside his narrow mouthparts, a tiny explosive bolt clicked into place. He aimed himself at the spinning tyre beside him. He didn't have the programming to work out exactly how fast the tyre was going, but it was a blur of movement.

With a decisive swoop, like a real mosquito moving in for a bite, Sabre dived at the tyre.

The wheel's speed was too much for his tiny frame. Instantly, he was bounced violently into the air before he could even attempt to inject the explosive,. He shot upwards, spinning out of control. The BMW revved and sped out of range.

For a few seconds, Sabre's systems were badly scrambled. He couldn't tell which way he was spinning, or where he was heading.

Miniature clamps suddenly caught hold of him. Chopper matched Sabre's wild mid-air spin, gripping the mosquito tightly. The two of them careered high over the road.

Gradually, Chopper's more powerful wings brought their flight under control and Sabre began to regain coordination of his sensors. Chopper stopped in mid-air, transmitted a stream of data back to base, and spun round. He headed for HQ, Sabre dangling limply beneath him.

Back at SWARM headquarters, Queen Bee switched off the screens and angrily squeezed her hands into fists. She swung her chair around. The people behind her were all looking shocked.

Finally, the silence was broken. "Well, well, well," said the head of MI5 with a sneer. "Better than normal agents, are they? I'm pretty sure my clumsy, obvious humans could have handled that rather more efficiently! Looks like your robots have let a dangerous weapon get into the wrong hands."

CHAPTER TWO

Deep beneath the streets of London, the top-secret headquarters of SWARM housed a network of rooms and passageways. On the lowest level of HQ was a long, narrow room with a low ceiling. The floor was a series of panels which shone a bright, slightly blue-tinted light throughout the room. Around the walls were display screens, machinery, files and racks of scientific equipment. Along the centre was a line of raised workbenches, some of them covered in a jumble of electronic circuits and wires. This was SWARM's laboratory.

At one of the benches, a young man was concentrating on his work. He was peering into a large, rectangular eyepiece, which stood out from a chunky machine in front of him. With each hand he manipulated what looked like an upside-down computer mouse. His expression was one of intense curiosity. Now and again, his hair flopped in front of his eyes and he flipped it clear.

Working opposite him was a much older man, tapping at the keys of a laptop. He wore a button-up cardigan and his hair was a wave of pure white.

The only sounds in the laboratory were the clicking of the keyboard and the low, gentle hum of power that pulsed through the machines.

When the young man spoke, his voice broke through the stillness of the room. "How's it going, Alfred?"

The old man scratched at his chin. He spoke with a distinct northern accent. "I know it sounds crazy, but I'm sure they've been writing their own subroutines into their core directories."

The young man didn't take his eyes off his

work, but shrugged. "That would account for their unexpected behaviour," he muttered.

Suddenly, the laboratory door opened and Professor Miller strode in. The Professor was a tall, thin man with a bald head. Behind him were a man and a woman, both smartly dressed.

"This is SWARM's laboratory," said the Professor in a gruff, no-nonsense tone. "I am in charge of the design and mechanics of our robots. I maintain their internal circuitry, perform upgrades and effect repairs."

He led them over to the young man. "Simon Turing here is our Data Analyst. His main tasks are to download and collate the data collected by our micro-robots, and to keep all members of SWARM up to date on current mission information."

The young man looked up and waved cheerily.

The Professor indicated the older man. "Alfred Berners is our Programmer," he said. "He created and maintains the robots' brain functions. He wrote the millions of lines of code which dictate the robots' behaviour, and develops subroutines which enhance or modify their response patterns. Mr Berners is one of the world's most distinguished scientists in the field of computer control systems."

"Hello," smiled Alfred Berners. "Has anyone seen my SD card with the test results on it?"

"Yes, I had it earlier," said Simon Turing, hopping off his stool.

Professor Miller tutted to himself when he noticed Simon's superhero T-shirt. "Mr Turing, Mr Berners," he said, introducing the man and woman he'd arrived with. "These people are our new field agents. Their role at SWARM is a small but important one. They will work alongside our robots, if and when required. At other times, they'll act as support here at headquarters. Agent J has been moved over from administrative duties at MI6," he explained, gesturing to the man standing with him, before turning to the woman and saying, "and this is Agent K, who comes to us from the CIA."

"Wow," said Simon, retrieving Alfred's SD card from a slot on a sleek electron microscope behind him. "You must have some great stories to tell."

"Nothing I can talk about," smiled Agent K. "Actually, I was on desk work at CIA headquarters in Langley, Virginia most of the time."

"Simon, have you downloaded the mission data from Chopper?" said the Professor.

"I was just doing it when you arrived," said Simon. "I think he got a look at one of those attackers, at least." He handed the SD card to Alfred.

The Professor nodded sharply. "Good. Ms Maynard will need your report as soon as possible. She's in the Home Secretary's office right now."

"After what happened this morning," said Alfred, placing the SD card in his laptop, "I wonder how our Queen Bee's getting on."

"I've never seen such a shambles in all my life!" shouted the Home Secretary.

Queen Bee shifted uncomfortably in her seat. The head of the Secret Intelligence Agency, her boss, was sitting on the Home Secretary's side of the huge oak desk, and was silent with red-faced embarrassment.

"Well?" cried the Home Secretary. "What are

you going to do about the situation? A top-secret weapon has been stolen by goodness-knows-who, I've got the Prime Minister demanding to know what's happening, and I can't even tell him exactly why it happened because SWARM doesn't officially exist!" She looked back and forth between Queen Bee and the SIA head. "You people make my blood boil!"

Queen Bee cleared her throat. She was every bit as angry as anyone at the loss of Whiplash, but she wouldn't let her emotions show. Especially now, when action was called for. She would never, she told herself, allow her feelings to cloud her judgement. She spoke as calmly as she could. "We're analysing the data recorded by Chopper, our dragonfly. We're confident of making a positive ID on one of the culprits soon."

"The sooner the better!" said the Home Secretary. "Didn't this Whiplash thing even have a homing tracker on it?"

"The risk was assessed as low, and the private company that—"

"Low risk? This is a top-secret project! And yet a bunch of crooks in a BMW knew about it.

Come to that, how did SWARM get involved?"

"It's our job to get involved, Home Secretary," said Queen Bee.

The Home Secretary stared angrily at her. "That's supposed to be an answer, is it?"

"It's all I'm authorized to say."

"To me?" cried the Home Secretary. "To me? I'm supposed to be in charge here! The intelligence agencies seem to think they have a right to—"

"Yes, but sometimes—" began Queen Bee.

"Don't interrupt me!" cried the Home Secretary. She shuffled the papers on her desk and took a deep breath. There was a great deal more to be said, and she wanted to say it as clearly and forcefully as possible.

Back in the underground SWARM laboratory, Simon Turing was making adjustments on a touchscreen while Professor Miller ran through the laboratory protocol with the new recruits.

"Queen Bee's probably got the Home

Secretary eating out of her hand," he muttered. "Or something. I try to keep clear of the political stuff." He turned to Agent J and Agent K. "Let me introduce you to the stars of our show."

He flipped a switch on the machine he'd been working at. The top section hissed gently as it opened, revealing a complicated mass of circuits and mechanical rods. In the middle of it all was Chopper, held in a delicate cage of tiny pincers. His wings shone in a hundred colours.

"The insects are all offline at the moment," said Simon, "so I can talk about them without them overhearing me and getting big-headed."

"You make them sound like humans," said Agent J.

Simon raised a finger. "Ah, hold that thought, we'll get back to it."

"That's amazing," gasped Agent K, leaning in for a closer look. "It looks like a real dragonfly."

"Of the order Odonata," said Alfred. "Beautiful creatures."

"Packed into that tiny shell," said Simon, "you've got telescopic-vision systems, scanning and recording units, even night vision and thermal-imaging capabilities. Ideal for surveillance and gathering information."

He pressed a button on the workbench, and a hatch beside it slid open. Inside was Sabre, hooked up to a set of miniature computers. "Sabre, our mosquito, got damaged on his recent mission. The Professor is in charge of mechanical and electronic components, he'll get him repaired and back to normal later today. Sabre is one of the smallest in the team, but he packs an almighty punch. Just as real mozzies bite, he can perform a range of stings and extractions. Carbon-fibre injection mechanisms built into his head can be pre-loaded with micro-pellets or used, for example, to test a target's blood."

Simon turned and tapped a six-digit number into a box on the wall. With a series of hums and whirs, five metallic cages rose up from the workbench, one by one. An insectoid robot was held in the middle of each, surrounded by circuitry and switches.

"Hercules," said Simon, indicating an oval-shaped stag beetle. "He's a heavy-duty agent. That serrated mouthpart claw can cut through solid metal, and he's tough enough to withstand a direct hit from a sledgehammer. He has an exoskeleton built from the latest in nano-fibre polymers, harder than diamond. As has Nero, our scorpion. You see that sting? That can deliver whatever chemical we give him. And his pincers make him our engineer, able to tap into electronics and carry out mechanical tasks."

Agent J and Agent K were staring at the robots with blank-faced astonishment. Simon smiled with pride and led them on to the next robot.

"Widow is our spider," he said. "She can produce threads and webs stronger than steel, and there's a communications array built into the abdomen that makes MI5 look like a satellite dish. Next, we have our centipede, Morph. He can dig, burrow and squeeze through spaces barely thicker than a sheet of paper, but his main attribute is his strength. Get him wrapped around your thumb and he could crush the bones inside it. Last, but certainly not least, we come to Sirena. She's a butterfly designed around a super-sensitive set of sensors. She's built as a kind of mobile analytical unit. She can detect all forms of air contamination, build up a detailed map of her immediate area, and even monitor the internal workings of a human being."

"You're calling them 'he' and 'she'," said Agent J. "Surely you're not going to tell me they have personalities?"

Simon grinned broadly. "They were only activated for the first time a matter of weeks ago, but they're already developing as distinct characters. This is where we come back to that point about humans. I think the sheer complexity of their programming has allowed them to have minds not unlike our own."

Professor Miller groaned loudly. "That's pure speculation. A few unexpected responses doesn't add up to a personality."

"Just before you came in," said Simon, "Fred was on to something, weren't you?"

"I know it sounds unlikely," said Alfred, running a hand through his white hair, "but I'm certain they're adding sections of code to their own programs. It's almost as if they're ... well, gaining memories, and experience."

"They're machines," blustered Professor

Miller. "Nothing more."

"They're some of the most advanced machines ever built," said Simon. "They're designed to think for themselves, it makes sense that they'd develop personalities, doesn't it? After all, we've given them names!"

"So, what are they like?" asked Agent K.

"Well," said Simon, "Chopper is the sensible one. If they were humans I'd call him their leader. Widow is a loner, an observer. Sabre, as you can probably tell from the way he charged in on that mission, tends to be a bit reckless. Hercules is the joker of the pack, Nero can be positively sarcastic at times, and Morph's a worrier, a bit unsure of himself. He's the last one to suggest anything rash."

"And Sirena?" asked Agent K.

"I think she's rather a mother figure," said Alfred. "She definitely keeps a watchful eye on the others."

"I can't wait to see these robots in action," said Agent J.

"Impressive, aren't they?" said Simon, like an excited kid.

"Speaking of action, let's return to the matter in hand," said Professor Miller. "I must make repairs to Sabre, and you, Simon, need to get Chopper's data analysed. I'm worried that Queen Bee will have some battles to fight inside our own organization as well as out in the real world."

"Relax, Prof," said Simon. "We're pioneers, we're ahead of our time, I'm sure we're here to stay."

The Home Secretary leaned across her desk and glared directly at Queen Bee. "If this Whiplash weapon isn't recovered within the next forty-eight hours, I'm closing the SWARM programme down. Is that clear? This Department of Microwave Whatever-it-is—"

"Micro-robotic Intelligence," interjected Queen Bee.

"—will be closed down before it's even got going. This meeting is over!"

CHAPTER THREE

At that same moment, the stolen metal case containing Whiplash was sitting on a battered-looking wooden table, located in a secret hideout. Standing around the table were fifteen men and women. Some were highly qualified scientists and the rest of the group were mercenaries, soldiers for hire, who wore khaki combat outfits and heavy boots.

The only light came from two bare electric bulbs, dangling on long wires. The large, dusty room was littered with packing crates and cardboard boxes.

"My heart's racing," murmured one of the scientists. "I've never got involved in anything like this before. I wasn't sure they'd actually do it."

"We're all in this together now," muttered another. "There's no going back."

"Aren't we going to open it, then?" called one of the men in combat gear.

Another of the uniformed men stepped forward, pulling a screwdriver from his pocket. He was short and heavily built, with a green kepi cap pulled tightly over his dark, straggly hair. He picked up the case and turned it around a few times, examining it. Then, with a couple of sniffs, he poised the screwdriver at a point where the two halves of the case met. Gritting his yellowing teeth, he dug the screwdriver into the join and began to lever it sharply. He grunted with effort. The case buckled slightly, but didn't break or open.

"Bullman!" cried a deep voice from behind him.

Everyone turned to see two figures enter the room. Bullman stopped what he was doing and stuck the screwdriver back into his pocket. His expression became sheepish. Nervously, he wiped the palms of his hands against his jacket.

All those gathered around the table fell silent.

The first of the two figures stepped forward, out of the darkness and into the pale glow of the hanging bulbs. His name was Williams, and his thick, pebble-like spectacles turned his eyes into dark, glittering globes. A thin smile split across his face.

The man he was with remained in the shadows. He was known to the group only as "the Insider". All they knew was that he had some kind of connection to the creation of Whiplash and that their operation depended on him.

Williams walked slowly over to Bullman, his shoes tapping on the concrete floor. Bullman drew back a little as he approached. Finally, Williams came to a halt with his nose barely three centimetres from Bullman's.

"Bullman," said Williams softly, in his Cockney accent, "I'd like you to reassure me."

Bullman blinked at him. "I d-don't quite follow you, boss," he stammered.

Williams's smile broadened. "I'd like you to reassure me. Put my mind at ease."

"W-what about, boss?"

"Couple of things," said Williams quietly. "Item one: you weren't really trying to break that case open with a screwdriver, were you? I mean, we've planned this robbery carefully, we've carried it out and now we've got the case, and inside it is an item worth millions and millions. You weren't really having a go at it with a screwdriver, were you, Bullman? If you were, then I'd separate your legs from your body using an assortment of garden tools. But you weren't, were you?"

"N-n-no, boss!" gabbled Bullman. "N-no way, boss, I w-was joking, boss, just mucking about."

Williams didn't move a muscle. His smile remained creepily wide and his voice remained calm. "That is good news, Bullman. I'm reassured on that point, thank you very much indeed. Now, item two: as I understand it, during the robbery, one of your boys fell over. Or fainted. Or something. Had to be carried back into the car. Could have ruined the whole thing. Reassure me that this was all down to the guy with the case being armed with a weapon. Reassure me that it's not a case of one of my squad being a wimp."

"I-i-it was Fraser!" cried Bullman, pointing to

another of the men dressed in combat gear. "Not me!"

Williams slowly turned his attention to the other man. Fraser suddenly felt an icy sensation run down his spine. No way was he going to admit that he thought he'd been stung by an insect!

"I was hit, Mr Williams!" cried Fraser. "Something hit me. Really hard. That guy must have stunned me with a Taser!"

"Did he?" said Williams softly. "Aw, that's all right, then." He paused for a moment, then suddenly clapped his hands together and let out a long, braying laugh. The tension in the room was broken. Everyone laughed and realized they'd barely taken a breath in the last couple of minutes.

"Come on, ladies and gentlemen," cried Williams, "we've got some celebrating to do!"

He picked up the metal case with one hand, and extended the other towards the mysterious man who was still lurking in the shadows. The Insider stepped forward and placed a small plastic card in Williams's outstretched hand.

Williams placed the card close to the handle

of the case. The card transmitted a code, and the case bleeped. It clicked and opened.

With great care, Williams lifted the lid of the case and removed Whiplash from where it rested in a smooth pad of protective plastic. Slightly smaller than a mobile phone, it was a plain brushed metal box with a set of connecting ports at one end and some words stamped in small black letters along the side.

"PROTOTYPE – copyright © Techna-Stik"

"Here it is," declared Williams, "the key to our future. This little box. We carry around a lot of little boxes, don't we? We talk to each other with them, we store our music on them, we watch telly on them. But this one is very different. This one is unlike any other on this precious planet of ours. Who would ever have thought that something this small could contain such power? And it's a power we now possess."

A murmured ripple of agreement went through the people standing around the table. In the pale light from the overhead bulbs, what could be seen of their faces showed a mixture of anticipation, apprehension and pride.

Williams continued. "In the crates and boxes stored in this room is all the equipment we've been quietly piecing together for many months. Today, our plans are complete. We have everything we need to put Operation New Age into effect!"

Everyone cheered.

Williams held Whiplash high above his head. "Ladies and gentlemen," he grinned, "we can begin!"

Queen Bee and her boss, the head of the UK's Secret Intelligence Agency, were arriving back at SWARM headquarters. They looked like business executives returning to their office, as they approached the bustle and noise of Trafalgar Square. None of the hundreds of people they passed had the slightest clue to their true identities, or to the dangerous problem they had to solve.

In the centre of Trafalgar Square stood Nelson's Column, rising high above the crowds and the traffic, as it had for over one hundred and eighty years. Briskly, they walked across to the fourth of the huge stone plinths that bordered the square. They stood at the sheltered lower corner of the plinth, beside a walled topped with a balustrade high above. Tucked away behind some benches was a spot few passers-by ever noticed.

They stood, as if quietly minding their own business, with their backs to the immense bulk of the plinth. Queen Bee glanced around, then touched her hand to the flat, cold stone. Palm-print recognition systems built into the stone verified who she was. In the blink of an eye, a holographic projector created a solid-looking image of the corner in front of them, masking them from view and giving the appearance of an empty corner.

Safely hidden from view, a narrow section of the plinth slid aside and they stepped inside. The slab settled back into place behind them, the projector switched off, and everything was back to normal.

Inside the plinth, Queen Bee and her boss had entered an elegantly designed lift. Queen Bee lifted her head slightly and spoke clearly. "This is Queen Bee, access T-alpha-324, confirm."

"Confirmed," said an electronic voice. The lift began to descend.

The head of the SIA's voice sounded muffled in the confines of the elevator. "You don't need me to tell you how serious the situation is."

"No, sir," said Queen Bee.

"I can't protect you, Beatrice. They'll shut you down unless those robots of yours succeed."

"Believe me, sir, I'm extremely angry, and extremely worried."

The head of the SIA shot a glance at her, his eyebrows raised. She seemed so calm.

The lift glided to a halt, and while the SIA chief headed deeper into the depths of the secret base, Queen Bee walked past the sliding doors marked "SWARM – Department Of Micro-robotic Intelligence" and headed for her office.

Once she was behind her desk, her calm mask dropped for a moment. She sat with her head in her hands, trying to clear her mind and think logically. At last she sat upright, pulled the hem of her jacket straight and tapped at the touchscreen in front of her. The face of Agent J, one of SWARM's new human agents, appeared on the screen.

"Online, Ms Maynard," said Agent J.

"Gather all SWARM staff for a briefing. We need results right now. And you, Agent J, I want you to go to Techna-Stik. They developed Whiplash, so they might have an angle on how to track it down that we don't know about. Sirena and Morph will accompany you."

"I'm live, Ms Maynard," said Agent J.

"We haven't a moment to lose." She tapped and the screen went blank.

"Any moment now, boss," said Bullman.

Williams nodded and waved him away. Bullman marched back across to where Fraser was working on Whiplash. The weapon was connected to a desktop computer and surrounded by a tangle of wires. The other members of the gang were busy unpacking equipment from crates and boxes.

Williams and the Insider were sitting on a

tatty leather sofa placed to one side of the hideout's large, dimly lit main room. The gang kept busy, respectfully leaving Williams alone unless summoned, and turning a blind eye to the Insider's presence, as instructed.

The Insider leaned over to Williams and whispered, "I should get back to Techna-Stik. They'll wonder where I am."

"Any problems there?" whispered Williams.

"I'm expecting a few secret service types to start snooping around soon, but there's nothing for them to find. There's nothing there to link me to … what did you call it, Operation New Age?"

Williams cracked his lizard-like smile. His eyes shone behind his thick spectacles. "Good name, don't you think? Makes this bunch of idiots think they're doing something noble."

"All I'm concerned about is making sure everything goes to plan," whispered the Insider. "I've got the bank hassling me for money."

"You deal with your side of things, I'll deal with mine."

"None of these people suspect the truth?"

Williams scanned the room and smiled to

himself. "No. Deluded halfwits. By the time the police turn up, we'll have got what we want and be well away."

"Aren't you worried about them seeking revenge?"

"From prison?" grinned Williams. "When they've no idea who you are, and they still think I'm a Londoner called Williams? Leave it out."

The Insider chuckled and patted him on the shoulder. "I really must go. Are you sure Fraser there can break into Whiplash's code? It's highly advanced stuff. Don't forget, I know all about the Whiplash project, but I can't bypass its security protocols. You need a technical genius."

"Stop fretting. Fraser and Bullman are eco-terrorist superstars! Fraser's the guy who hacked into the FBI's central computers in America last month and put a smiley face on their website. There's nothing he can't crack."

At that moment, Fraser looked up from his computer. "Boss? I … I don't think I can crack it."

Williams launched himself from the sofa and strode across the room. "What? What did you say?"

"Look at this," pleaded Fraser. "There's, like,

a six-terabit encryption module embedded on the main CPU chip."

"And translated from the Geek, that means…?" growled Williams.

"It means you need a code just to switch Whiplash on, let alone fire it. And working out what that code is could take months."

"What?" bellowed Williams.

"Maybe even years."

"Years?"

"There's no way around it, boss. I keep coming up against something called an AKA number. I don't even know what that means!"

"AKA," said the first technician, "stands for Activation Keycode Authorization."

On the twelfth floor of the glass tower that housed the UK offices of Techna-Stik International, two technicians were fussing around SWARM's Agent J. Their workshop was possibly the untidiest place Agent J had ever seen, the exact opposite of SWARM's gleaming, state-of-the-art lab. The entire room was a mass of bleeping, flashing machinery, as eccentric and geeky as the technicians who worked in it. Outside the enormous windows was a spectacular view across London.

Agent J casually placed his smartphone on a cluttered table and entered a code on its keypad, causing a small flap to hum open in its side. As he talked with the two technicians, distracting their attention, Sirena the butterfly and Morph the centipede silently emerged from the phone, Sirena uncurling her wings as she crawled out into the open. She took up a position above the window, her sensors decrypting the room's Wi-Fi signal, while Morph used connectors in four of his legs to plug into a networked tablet left on a nearby chair.

"We developed AKA ourselves," said the first technician, Philip Jones.

"How does it work?" asked Agent J.

Jones and the second technician, Lewis Macarthur, hurried back and forth producing circuit diagrams and computer readouts. Their identical white lab coats were dotted with a variety of food and coffee stains.

"It's like a time lock on a bank vault," said Jones, pushing his glasses back along the bridge of his nose.

"A time-locked vault will only open at certain times," said Macarthur.

"And even the bank staff can't open it unless it's at a pre-set opening time," said Jones. "For maximum security."

"Our AKA system works the same way," said Macarthur.

"You have to pre-program when you want Whiplash to be unlocked," said Jones. "At any other time it won't even switch on. And to pre-program those times, you currently need pretty much all the equipment you can see in this workshop, plus thumbprint IDs from the two of us, plus a retina scan from Mr Haynes—"

"He's UK Operations Director, he's in charge here," said Macarthur.

"—and also from Mr Oliphant," said Jones. "He's the company's Head of Projects."

Agent J nodded. "So you had Whiplash pre-programmed to operate first thing this morning, when the meeting at the Ministry of Defence was going to take place. But, of course, Whiplash was stolen, and the meeting never happened, so now Whiplash will be locked again. Yes?"

"That's right," said Macarthur. "The only way to switch Whiplash on now is to crack its AKA code. And that could take someone months."

"Or even years," said Jones. "We take Whiplash's security extremely seriously."

"Extremely seriously," echoed Macarthur.

"Because it's a very dangerous bit of kit," said Jones.

"And you're confident that the code can't be worked out?" said Agent J.

The two technicians sniggered and snorted to themselves. "You'd need to be a mathematics genius, and an expert in cryptography," said Jones.

"That means code-breaking," said Macarthur. "You'd need to be way cleverer than us."

"Way cleverer," said Jones.

"And that's not going to happen, is it?" said Macarthur. The two of them giggled and jostled each other.

Agent J closed his eyes and let out a long, slow breath. "Excuse me a moment," he said. He picked up his phone, moved away and tapped into the SWARM micro-robots' internal communications network. Jones and Macarthur busied themselves with the mass of machinery.

"How's it going?" said Agent J in a low voice.

"They really do take security seriously," said Sirena. "We've tapped into all the company's systems, and it seems that every record of the Whiplash project is held electronically, behind an alarmed firewall. There's nothing on paper at all."

"What if something happened to their data?" said Morph. "They'd have no written backup. That's not a sensible idea, is it?"

"No, it's a bit odd," said Agent J. "Have you got the files?"

"Affirmative," said Sirena. "The firewall presented no problem. I'm transmitting the entire Whiplash database back to HQ now."

"Good work," said Agent J. "Anything else?"

"We've analyzed information about the project and all the people employed here," said Morph, "and we've reached a worrying conclusion. We're almost certain that someone inside Techna-Stik is working with the people who stole Whiplash."

"Any idea who?" said Agent J.

"Wait," said Sirena. "Sensor readings show two humans are approaching this room."

At that moment, the workshop door hummed open and in came Mr Haynes and Mr Oliphant. Agent J put the call on hold.

Mr Haynes, Techna-Stik's UK Operations Director, was a middle-aged man with a deeply lined face and hooded eyes. Oliphant's thin features looked drawn and tired. He was still feeling shaky from that morning's attack. The technicians introduced them to Agent J.

"You're from MI5?" said Mr Haynes.

"Yes," lied Agent J. He showed Mr Haynes his fake ID.

Mr Haynes looked around. "Well, where are the others? I asked for a whole team to be put on this! Spies, police, the lot! Do you realize how serious this theft is?"

"I'm sure they do," said Mr Oliphant with a touch of impatience. "We all do."

"Everything possible is being done," said Agent J. "As we speak, there are undercover agents assigned to the weapon's recovery. What I'm more concerned about is the fact that the thieves must surely have had inside help."

Mr Haynes shook his head angrily. "Everyone working on the Whiplash project was checked and re-checked. Everyone, even me! Police checks, background checks, every possible check you can think of. If they'd checked our dental records it wouldn't have surprised me!"

"I can't believe any member of staff here would do such a thing," said Mr Oliphant. "They'd have to be desperate. You can't exactly sell a weapon like Whiplash to some local crook."

"The fact remains," said Agent J, "that the thieves not only found out about Whiplash, but knew exactly when it would leave this building. I assume you protect this place from listening devices and cameras?"

"We have detectors in every room," said Haynes. "I wouldn't put anything past those swine at Gylbut Gadgets. They're our main business rivals. But the staff here are loyal to the company.

Techna-Stik is a major international corporation.
We pay our workers well, and we look after them
like family. It doesn't make sense!"

"I'll do some checking of my own, if I may,"
said Agent J.

"Yes," said Mr Haynes. "If Whiplash isn't found
fast, it won't only be me who loses his job! Now,
if you'll excuse me, I have work to do."

He left the room, Oliphant trailing along behind
him. Jones and Macathur returned to their work.
Agent J returned to his conversation with the
micro-robots.

"Suspects?" said Agent J quietly, watching
Jones and Macarthur adjust an oscilloscope.
Ripples of high-pitched sound bounced across
the workshop as they twisted its dials.

"There are twelve Techna-Stik personnel who
fit more than a few of the search parameters,"
said Morph. "We checked against police records,
employment histories, known access to Whiplash,
and thirty-three other factors."

"Only four are likely suspects," said Sirena.
"Technicians John Jones and Lewis Macarthur,
Head of Projects Marcus Oliphant and UK

Operations Director William Haynes."

"However," said Morph, "none of these four match enough parameters to make a positive ID on who is cooperating with the thieves. To begin with, none of them appears to have any motive for the crime. None whatsoever. As Mr Haynes said, Techna-Stik's employees are loyal to the company."

"Jones and Macarthur certainly seem unlikely crooks," muttered Agent J. "Haynes would surely gain far more by selling Whiplash to the Ministry of Defence than risking his job and his company's future by allowing it to be stolen. So he doesn't seem likely either. And Oliphant was the one who got robbed this morning."

"That could have been staged," suggested Sirena.

"Why?" said Agent J. "He didn't know SWARM was watching. Why fake a robbery, when you could just hand Whiplash over?"

"Perhaps he correctly assumed that the secret services would be taking an interest," said Sirena. "The only thing we can say for certain is that we need more information!"

At that moment, three floors above, Haynes and Oliphant were making their way to a routine management meeting. Their footsteps were silent in the thickly carpeted corridor, and they spoke in low voices.

Haynes eyed Oliphant glumly. "The company might be in serious trouble here. As if there wasn't enough to worry about!"

Oliphant's phone began to ring. "I'll catch you up in a minute," he mumbled.

For a moment or two, Oliphant watched Mr Haynes marching away down the corridor, then he tapped at his phone. The call was one he'd been dreading. As soon as he heard the voice on the line, he began to sweat.

"Yes, I know," he answered, his voice shaking slightly.

"I'm afraid we still haven't received the payment you promised us last week," said the woman. "You do understand what will happen if there are further defaults on these loans? I believe that my colleague here at the bank went through the procedure with you?"

"Yes."

"I'm really sorry, Mr Oliphant, but we can only give you a few more days. After that, the bank will be forced to repossess your house, cars and other assets to clear the debt. We really must have a large repayment of money as soon as possible."

"Yes," said Mr Oliphant. "I understand."

"I'm sorry, we have no other choice. We'll be in touch."

Mr Oliphant tapped shakily at his phone, then dabbed his forehead with a handkerchief.

Back in the laboratory at SWARM headquarters, Professor Miller and Simon Turing were closely examining a stream of data files that Simon had retrieved from Chopper the dragonfly's memory. The files contained masses of information gathered during the theft of Whiplash.

"This is the best we've got," said Simon. He reached across the 3D computer display that hung in mid-air above one of the workbenches. A set of virtual folders swirled around in the blue haze of the display until, with a twist of Simon's hand, a single file separated out from the others.

It swung upright to reveal a blurred photograph of a face.

"It was taken at high speed," said Simon, "so there's rather a lot of blurring, but this guy must have taken off his balaclava and looked around. He was in the front passenger seat of the BMW, I think he was checking to see if the car was being followed. Do you see?"

Professor Miller nodded. His bald head seemed to glow pale blue in the light from the computer display. "This is the only shot of a face we have?" he asked.

"Yes, Chopper was trying to keep tabs on all the thieves at once and fly close enough to the car to gather data. He was lucky to get this, to be honest."

"Let's see what the Secret Intelligence Agency's database makes of it," said the Professor. He tapped at a nearby keyboard.

The 3D display bleeped and the photo was

suddenly surrounded by a series of lines and numbers. Hundreds of faces flashed past at lightning speed. The image was being cross-checked against the information held by the SIA on known crooks and terrorists.

Simon Turing waited nervously, his fingers tapping at the workbench. A few seconds later, the display bleeped twice and a section of text scrolled up in front of Simon's eyes, along with newspaper clippings and more photos.

"Bingo!" declared Simon with a grin. "Our suspect's name is Michael Kevin Bullman."

MICHAEL KEVIN BULLMAN

D.O.B: 11/07/75
Height: 170cm
Appearance: Caucasian
Heavy build
Dark Hair

CAREFILE:
• Eco-terrorism
involvement - ongoing
• Arrests
07/06/96
Released without charge
01/02/99
Convicted of arson
• Open cases
Malaysia - Dam case
insufficient evidence
Paris Office case -
insufficient evidence

The Professor stood at Simon's shoulder.

"Known eco-terrorist and mercenary," continued Simon. "He's run various gangs and paramilitary squads in the past. He's got a police file as long as a giraffe's neck, and he's currently wanted in connection with the destruction of a dam in Malaysia and the burning down of an office block in Paris."

The Professor was already calling Queen Bee's number at the communicator on the wall. "Any associates?" he said.

D.O.B: 21/01/87
Height: 184cm
Appearance: Caucasian

AUGUSTUS TIBERIUS FRASER

D.O.B: 21/01/87
Height: 184cm
Appearance: Caucasian
          Slim
          Blond

CAREFILE:
• Eco-terrorism
involvement - ongoing
• Suspected hacker of F.B.I.
central database
No charges -
insufficient evidence
• Linked to multiple fraud
and identity theft cases -
insufficient evidence

"Several," said Simon, reading from the display. "Most notably Augustus Tiberius Fraser. What a name!"

Queen Bee's face appeared on the 3D display. The Professor told her what they'd discovered.

"Good work!" said Queen Bee. "Look for location leads. Are there any unusual properties listed against this Bullman? Somewhere the gang might be using to hide Whiplash?"

Simon quickly checked through the data, one finger scrolling the text inside the display. "He's listed as having no fixed address, as such. Although... Ah! In the last week he's started renting a large lock-up beneath a railway arch just south of the River Thames, near Vauxhall Cross. Using a fake ID, of course."

"That's where they'll be," said Queen Bee.

"If we make a move on them," said Simon, "we'll really annoy the cops. According to this data, they got wise to the fake ID and are preparing to raid the place themselves."

"Tough," said Queen Bee. "Recovering Whiplash is more important. We must move in before the police do."

"Logged, Queen Bee," said Simon.

Queen Bee's face loomed large in the display. "Mission objective is to detain our suspects and recover Whiplash," she said. "Launch the SWARM!"

CHAPTER FOUR

A computerized voice spoke from the ceiling. "Active mode authorized. Micro-agents online."

"I'm live," said Chopper the dragonfly.

"I'm live," came the deeper, slower voice of Hercules the stag beetle.

The SWARM robots' high-tech, cage-like boxes glided up out of the workbench. Each was brightly lit from inside. Tiny red and green lights flashed in sequence and a hum of power pulsed through the room.

One by one, the insectoid robots activated. Legs flexed, antennae twitched.

"I'm live," each of the robots said in turn: Widow the spider; Nero the scorpion; Morph the centipede; Sirena the butterfly; and Sabre the mosquito, now fully repaired.

The cages slid open and the SWARM emerged on to the workbench.

Simon grinned at the Professor. "Those bad guys won't know what hit them."

In their hideout, the members of Operation New Age had nearly finished unpacking the crates and boxes, and were busy connecting and setting up the equipment they'd need to put their plan into effect.

Fraser the computer hacker was still sitting in front of his desktop PC, trying to break into the AKA code protecting Whiplash. Sweat beaded on his forehead and he was getting more irritated and anxious with every passing minute.

Williams appeared at his shoulder. Fraser deliberately kept his gaze on the screen in front of him.

"Well, any progress?" demanded Williams.

"None whatsoever!" spat Fraser angrily.

Williams lowered his face level with Fraser's and spoke very quietly. "That's not what I want to hear. If you're no good to us, you're going to get kicked off this project. Remember what'll happen to anyone we have to kick off this project? Straight into the river wearing concrete wellies."

Fraser gulped and tried to stop his hands shaking as they hovered over the keyboard. "Why didn't the Insider warn us about this coded security?" he moaned.

"He did," said Williams through gritted teeth. "And your mate Bullman promised me you wouldn't find it a problem."

Fraser wiped the sweat off his face with the grubby sleeve of his combat jacket. "Well, it is a problem!"

At that moment, Bullman entered the room carrying a large cardboard box filled with tinned and dried food. With a grunt, he dropped it on to a table. The sudden thump made Fraser jump.

"Any trouble on the way in?" said Williams.

"Naaah!" scoffed Bullman. "I've told you,

boss, there's no way anyone will find us here. A perfect hiding place like this?"

Agent K, one of the new SWARM agents, made her way down a narrow alley. She had crossed the Thames at Westminster Bridge and walked through a series of backstreets and underpasses until she reached the rundown area. Bits of paper and empty fast-food wrappers blew along the gutter, and she could hear a dog barking menacingly in the distance.

She emerged from the alleyway into a large derelict patch of land. To one side was a hill of rubble and rubbish, beyond which she could see the towering buildings north of the river. In front of her was a wide area of scrubby brown grass, dotted with bricks and surrounded by an expanse of gravel. Opposite was the tall shape of a railway viaduct, blackened and crumbling with age.

Beneath the viaduct was a series of huge arches, each more than ten metres high. The arches were filled with walls of shabby, rotting wood. Some of the walls had signs clinging on to them. In chipped and faded paint they announced things like "G&I Motors – brakes, tyres, exhausts" and "Butler's Wholesale Fish – fresh today!".

The place was eerily quiet – there was no sound except for the distant roar of traffic and the continued barking of somebody's dog. Agent K crouched down, and took a silver case from her inside jacket pocket. Carefully, she placed it on the grass in front of her and stood back.

The case suddenly flipped open, and SWARM's seven micro-robots emerged. Each of them beeped a contact signal back to SWARM headquarters, where Queen Bee watched seven monitors.

The screens showed a complex array of information, including the robots' exact locations, the programming subroutines that were guiding their behaviour, and the current status of their sensor readings. The largest section of each display was taken up with a view of what the robots were seeing. The advanced cameras fitted into Chopper showed the clearest picture, since he was designed to record and observe in fine detail.

Crouched on the grass, Agent K snapped the case shut and, pausing only to make sure she wasn't being followed, she stood and made her way back to the road.

The robots maintained their positions.

"Get ready to move in," said Queen Bee.

"I can't do it," declared Fraser, slumping over the keyboard of his PC and gripping it with sweating hands. "Every route through the program ends in a lockout." On the screen in front of him, multiple terminal windows showed long strings of UNIX commands, each ending in error codes. "The Whiplash software continually rewrites the encryption algorithm. You'd have to think three dozen steps ahead of it all the time!"

Williams looked from Fraser to the PC's screen and back again. He took in a long, slow breath.

With a sudden knotted feeling in his stomach, Fraser realized he'd pushed too far.

Everyone in the room carried on with what they were doing but kept one eye on Williams, wondering what he would do.

Williams stood beside Fraser. "Oh … dear … me," he said quietly. "Are you telling me you can't do your job? Is that what you're telling me?"

He loomed over Fraser, blocking out the light from the bare electric bulb hanging high above. Fraser stared up at Williams, terrified.

"Move in," said the voice of Queen Bee in the robots' sensory circuits. "Detain the suspects and locate the weapon."

"I'm live, Queen Bee," signalled Chopper. He transmitted a stream of data to the other robots: "Spread out. Sensors on maximum. Our target is the lock-up in the middle."

"We'll make a beeline for it," said the deep voice of Hercules.

"Very, very funny, Hercules," said Nero. "What great programming."

"Pay attention," came the high, musical voice of Sirena the butterfly. "We have a job to do. Queen Bee, are you getting my data feed?"

"Got it," said Queen Bee back at headquarters, checking Sirena's monitor. It was filled with sensor readings of the area surrounding the butterfly.

All seven robots moved ahead at speed. Sirena, Chopper the dragonfly, Hercules the stag beetle and Sabre the mosquito flew low over the grass, fanning out slightly so that their sensors could pick up information from a wider area. Nero the scorpion, Widow the spider and Morph the centipede scuttled rapidly across the ground.

"How many suspects will there be?" said Morph. "What weapons will they have?"

"Unknown, as yet," said Chopper. "Stay alert."

Sirena, whose sensors were the most advanced, fluttered a little ahead of the others. The long antennae extending from her head waved and turned to pick up whatever clues she could.

"I'm detecting life forms in the lock-up," she said.

"How many?" said Chopper.

"Processing…" said Sirena. "Multiple life signals, but the trace is quite faint. I don't detect anything shielding my signals. Not sure what to make of it."

"There could be electronic interference," said Chopper.

"That would match with the suspects' likely behaviour patterns," said Nero, his circuits checking against the information downloaded by Simon.

They were twenty metres from the lock-up and closing in.

"Widow, block the escape route," said Chopper.

"Logged," said the clipped voice of the spider.

Widow fired a thin strand of web ahead of her and swung at lightning speed, landing neatly on the wooden planks that formed the wall beneath the archway. Her legs gripping the wood with micro-hooks, she turned to face the wide, hefty door built into the wall.

With rapid jumps and twists, she leaped back and forth from one side of the door to the other. Behind her, she left a continuous line of thread, narrower than a human hair, but twice as strong as steel cable. Within a minute, a perfect crosshatched web had been formed across the door. Anyone trying to leave the lock-up would find their way barred.

"Exit sealed," she said.

By now, the others had caught up with her.

"Attack mode," said Chopper. "Nero, remain on guard out here. Other agents, prepare for combat."

The robots quickly made their way round or through the wooden wall, creeping through tiny gaps and cracks. Hercules's saw-like mouthparts cut a tiny tunnel at ground level. Morph squashed himself almost flat and squeezed underneath a large section of planking.

"I hope they don't try to stamp on me," said the centipede.

Seconds later, they were inside. The lock-up was cavernous and dark. The robots' sensors picked up damp and decay.

This was no hideout. It was empty.

"Scan," said Chopper. The night-vision filters in his eye cameras took in the dusty floor and the curved brick ceiling high above. Sirena's antennae analyzed the air. Dozens of rats scurried about, their long tails scraping along behind them, darting in an out of holes in the ancient brickwork.

"Those rats were the life forms I detected," said Sirena. "There was no electrical interference."

Chopper's eye cameras zoomed in on the floor below. They flipped through night-vision, infra-red and ultra-violet modes. "There are marks in the dust everywhere. Rectangular shapes and lines."

Queen Bee stood at SWARM headquarters, eyes fixed on the data as it streamed across the screens.

"Logically, I'd say someone was storing a lot of boxes here," said Sabre.

"The marks get disturbed when the rodents run across them," said Chopper, watching a large rat cross the floor. "Since most of the marks are not disturbed, the boxes must have been here very recently."

Sirena took readings of the rats' movements and made some calculations. "Based on the number of rodents present, the boxes were moved within the past two days."

"Have the suspects moved their hideout?" asked Morph.

"No, the people who stole Whiplash were only storing things here temporarily," said Chopper. "The theft happened nine hours, forty-three minutes ago. The thieves probably believe the police and secret service still don't know who they are, or where they are, so they are unlikely to have decamped."

The robots scanned for forensic evidence: DNA, clothing fibres and other traces that might lead them to the gang. All that was found were some fingerprints on the door, belonging to Bullman.

"He's already a target," said Chopper. "We're no further forward in our investigation."

"And time is running out," muttered Queen Bee, back at SWARM headquarters.

Williams's hand was gripped tightly around the collar of Fraser's combat jacket.

"Well?" barked Williams.

"I'm sorry, boss, I just can't do it," whined Fraser.

"Do you want me to lose my patience with you? Huh? Do you?"

"The coding that protects Whiplash needs a mathematical genius to crack it. I'm the best hacker there is, you know that, boss, but this is Einstein-level. It isn't possible for me, but … but … it might be possible for someone else."

Behind his thick spectacles, Williams's eyes narrowed. "Meaning…?"

"I've got an idea, boss," said Fraser, squirming. "I think I know who can crack that code. It'll only mean a short delay to the project. A few hours, tops. I need to go out for a while. Me, and Bullman, and a couple of heavies. Is that OK? Boss? OK?"

Slowly, Williams relaxed his grip on Fraser and stood back. Fraser hurriedly straightened his collar. The other members of Operation New Age watched them expectantly.

Williams sniffed. "OK," he said quietly. "I want you back here before sunrise. And keep a sharp eye out when you're coming and going. Our presence here is supposed to be secret, remember. Minimum movement outside."

"Yes, boss. I understand, boss," gulped Fraser.

Bullman had been sitting on the battered leather sofa in the corner, watching Fraser's discomfort with a mixture of sympathy and amusement on his face. Now he got up and whistled over to two of the gang members in combat gear.

The four men prepared to leave, Fraser keeping a watchful eye on Williams all the time. The room had a hefty metal door with large rivets around its edges. In the middle of the door was a big red wheel.

Bullman turned the wheel anti-clockwise, and swung the door back on its fat hinges. Beyond the door was a gloomy concrete corridor. Dim lights were set into the walls at wide intervals, behind damage-resistant iron frames.

The door closed behind the four men with a loud clang. The wheel spun until the door was firmly locked again.

CHAPTER FIVE

"So, we have no idea where their base of operations is?" said Alfred.

The programmer was walking along the main corridor of SWARM HQ. To either side were offices, workshops and emergency living quarters.

Beside him strode Queen Bee, and between them flew Chopper the dragonfly and Hercules the stag beetle, their precise mechanical wings keeping them exactly at Alfred's eye level.

"I'm afraid not," said Queen Bee.

Alfred shrugged. "Don't worry, there must be some way for us to find them. Chopper, were there any other clues left at the lock-up?"

"Negative, Alfred," said Chopper.

"Simon has downloaded all the data we collected," said Hercules, "but it contains no new information. He has also checked the data gathered by Agent J, Sirena and Morph, over at Techna-Stik, but we have no clues as to the identity of the informer."

"Whoever at Techna-Stik is working with this gang," muttered Queen Bee, "they've covered their tracks very well."

"Hmm," said Alfred, frowning. "Let's think now. The thieves have obviously gone to a lot of trouble to steal Whiplash. If they're smart enough to plan the robbery, they're smart enough to realize that right now they're top priority for MI5, and so on. Right?"

"Right," said Queen Bee.

"So," said Alfred, "if they're prepared to turn themselves into such a significant target, then they must have pretty big plans for Whiplash."

"Clearly, yes," said Queen Bee. "Where exactly does it lead us, though?"

"As I see it, there can only be three possible

reasons why they stole Whiplash. The first is that they're simply holding it to ransom. Give us a huge pile of cash or we bash it to bits, that sort of thing. But if that was their motive, then we'd surely have heard about it by now. They'd have contacted the police, or someone, and issued their demands. After all, they would need to get rid of the device as soon as possible. The longer they have Whiplash in their possession, the greater the chance that we'll catch them red-handed. But they've had Whiplash for a whole day and we haven't heard from them."

"What's the second reason?" said Queen Bee. "That they're going to sell it, I presume?"

"Exactly," said Alfred.

"Who would they sell it to?" said Hercules. "A foreign government, perhaps?"

"Or a terrorist group?" added Chopper.

"Yes, if that was indeed why they stole it," said Alfred. "But I doubt that's really their motive. The one clue we have is that this Bullman character is involved. And possibly so are friends of his such as … what was his name? Fraser! Bullman and Fraser are known fanatics. They try to destroy businesses, embarrass officials, ruin projects they don't agree with. They're a bunch of thugs, but they think they're fighting for a cause. Their attitude is: if we don't like it, we'll wreck it. I seriously doubt people like that would have stolen Whiplash just to pass it on. Would they really get hold of a massively powerful weapon in order to flog it?"

"That makes sense," nodded Queen Bee. "Which leads us to the third reason – they're going to activate it themselves."

"Spot on," said Alfred. "They stole it to use it. But Whiplash still hasn't been fired. We'd certainly know if it had! That might suggest they're not actually capable of firing it. At least, not yet."

"Couldn't they be transporting it somewhere?" said Chopper. "They might intend to fire it on the other side of the world."

"Transporting it would be another big risk," said Alfred. "Lots of chances to get caught. What they're planning can't be like any terrorist outrage ever before. It's Whiplash they've stolen, a very specific weapon that does a very specific thing. They want it because this time, bombs and guns aren't good enough. I think we can be reasonably sure that, just at the moment, they don't know how to fire it. All that security built into the weapon is keeping them out. They can't break the AKA code."

"But if Fraser is involved," said Queen Bee, "why are they having difficulty? He's one of the world's top computer hackers."

"Agent J sent me the details of Techna-Stik's AKA system after his visit there," said Alfred. "There's no way even I could crack it, and I'm the cleverest person I know. Well, given a few weeks I might crack it. But the thieves haven't got a few weeks. They know we'll track them down eventually. They can't afford to delay for even twenty-four hours, let alone any longer."

"So they'll need help from outside," concluded Queen Bee. "Brilliant! Chopper, Hercules, access the main databanks. Find information on anyone who might be able to crack that code without breaking a sweat. Mathematicians, cryptographers, anyone. Cross reference by geographical location."

"We're live, Queen Bee," said the two robots.

They beamed a login signal to the mainframe computer on the floor below.

"Search successful," said Chopper. "Four possible candidates found. Two are out of the country, one lives in northern Scotland. The most likely person for the gang to contact is Dr Madeleine Smith, lecturer in Applied Mathematics at the University of South Warwickshire."

"Good work," said Queen Bee. "Alfred, tell Professor Miller to prepare the SWARM. We'll send a team to guard Dr Smith immediately."

In the thieves' hideout, over a dozen members of the gang were seated in two rows, facing a fold-out projection screen that had been rigged up at one end of the room. Their leader Williams was connecting a laptop to a projector. The mysterious Insider, the gang's contact inside Techna-Stik, had returned from the Techna-Stik offices and sat to one side of the screen, in the shadows behind Williams.

The gang members talked quietly amongst

themselves until at last Williams raised a hand for silence. He pressed a small remote control and a series of graphics and photos filled the screen as he spoke.

"The time has come," he announced. "This is your final briefing before Operation New Age is put into effect." He flashed his lizard-like smile at his audience, his dark eyes shining behind the thick lenses of his spectacles.

"Mr Bullman and his team will return soon," he continued, "and the problem of cracking Whiplash's code should be solved within hours. Once that minor inconvenience is overcome, we can begin!"

A ripple of approval went through the gang.

"I am a hard taskmaster, you all know that. But it's because I care so passionately about Operation New Age and all it stands for. We are united as a group in our desire to see the world reborn."

The group applauded.

Williams spoke more softly. "I'd like to thank each and every one of you. For your contributions to the project. For your time, your commitment and, yes, your money. Operation New Age has been largely funded, as you are aware, through our friend here..."

He extended a hand towards the Insider. There was more applause, which the Insider acknowledged with a nod.

"But all of you have given generously, to allow us to assemble the equipment you see around us now. Equipment that will, in due course, be dismantled and destroyed, once the New Age has finally dawned. We'll burn it, when it's no longer needed, when it's useless in our new world. How ironic, how amusing, that the Earth will be changed forever using this machinery. Mankind's technology will be the cause of its own destruction!"

There were cries of support and raised fists.

Williams eyed them all, smiling. "Here, then, is the plan. Phase One begins with the firing of Whiplash, from right where we are now. In here, we are safe from Whiplash's devastating effects. This bunker is the only one of its kind – its construction was top secret and it has been designed to withstand atomic warfare. Our assembled equipment will amplify Whiplash's power a thousand times. A massive EMP, a huge electro-magnetic pulse, will radiate out for almost eighty miles. All of Greater London will be hit, the whole south-east of England will feel Whiplash's mighty hammer-blow, its shattering blast! And yet … no explosion, no heaps of rubble. The blow will be silent. Instant. No human being will even know it's happened, until they see its effects. Every last electronic circuit, fried and useless. No more TVs spouting rubbish, no more cyber-bullying, no more cars and factories filling the air with filth."

The gang cheered loudly.

Williams raised a hand for silence again. "You all know your individual tasks. Each of you is a trained scientist, that's why you've been chosen for Operation New Age. Every last one of you has a vital part to play, either operating Whiplash's amplifier, or monitoring its effects, or preparing Phase Two. This second phase is the most important. While the world outside is in confusion, our hideout will be the focal point for a global switch-off. This place has many rooms, it's big enough for us to live in while our plans are carried out."

One of the gang members spoke up. He was a tall, thin man with prominent teeth. "Mr Williams, how can we be sure the authorities won't find us?"

"Phase Two will take about a week," said Williams.

The screen behind him flickered and changed to a map of the world overlaid with large circles. "The chaos of Phase One will give the authorities so much to deal with that we can count on a few weeks of safety. They'll have no phones, no vehicles, no nothing."

"But what if the authorities have some kind of shielding against it?" asked the thin man nervously.

"Whiplash is the first and only one of its kind," said Williams. "Asking if they've got shielding is like expecting a caveman to be wearing a bullet-proof vest! There is, as yet, no defence against Whiplash."

"Except right here where we are?"

"Correct. And the authorities couldn't make a Whiplash of their own anyway. The Insider has made sure that all Techna-Stik's records of the project are computerized. Nothing exists on paper. So, when the weapon is fired: bang! Techna-Stik's computers will be trashed, and anyone wanting to create a similar weapon would have to start from scratch. It took Techna-Stik ten years to develop Whiplash."

Williams exchanged a knowing glance with the Insider.

"Phase Two," declared Williams, the screen behind him showing a series of locations and statistics, "will see Whiplash targeted at every major city on earth, and then at the rest of the planet's surface. The whole world will be switched off. The New Age will dawn!"

"Mankind will revert to a simpler time, before technology took over our lives and our environment was ravaged by industry! Horse-drawn wagons for transport, everyone growing their own food, a healthier, quieter way of life for us all. No pollution, no energy crisis, no threat of global war. Now, as you know, when Whiplash strikes there will be problems. Lorries will crash, aeroplanes will fall from the sky, hospitals will lose power. There will be deaths. But remember our ultimate goal. In war, there are always casualties. Some will die, but the whole of mankind will benefit. Now, let's get back to work."

There was more applause and cheering. Despite the knowledge that Operation New Age would cause death and destruction, the group had persuaded themselves that they were fighting for a cause. They believed that someone had to create a better world by force!

As the gang returned to their preparations, Williams sat in the shadows beside the Insider.

"Very impressive speech," whispered the Insider. "You almost had me believing it myself. Do we really need to tell them all that rubbish about a Phase Two?"

"We need them to work. We need to keep them on our side. If they knew that Phase Two isn't going to happen, and that this entire operation is only a way of making money for you and me, do you really think they'd be here now? We need scientific experts to assemble and operate the machinery. They're interested in helping the planet, not making a profit, so the deception is vital. By the time they realize they've been duped, we'll be well away."

"I've been talking with my people at Gylbut Gadgets," whispered the Insider. "They're nearly ready to start making Whiplash shielding. I'll be able to switch the whole company over to shielding production once the Whiplash is fired. With the whole world terrified of another attack, we'll be billionaires."

"And in the meantime," smiled Williams, watching the gang at work, "this bunch of gullible idiots will be left high and dry." He looked at his wristwatch. "Bullman should be there by now."

CHAPTER SIX

The grandfather clock in the hall ticked its way towards 11:30pm. The house was an old one, with low ceilings crossed by thick wooden beams, just outside a quiet little village, several miles from the nearest town.

In the downstairs study, Dr Madeleine Smith, lecturer in Applied Mathematics at the University of South Warwickshire, was working at a large antique desk. The study was lined with bookcases and filing cabinets. On the walls were paintings, photographs and academic certificates.

Dr Smith herself was elegantly dressed. Her

cascade of brown hair fell around delicate features and large eyes. She was noting a long series of mathematical formulae on a tablet computer.

She sat back, eyeing her work carefully. Her mouth twisted into an uncertain expression. Pushing her chair back, she yawned loudly, stood up and left the room.

The moment she was gone, one of the paintings on the study wall appeared to come to life. It was a picture of a summer meadow, dotted with butterflies. One of the butterflies suddenly flexed its wings and fluttered off the frame.

Sirena sent out a signal. "All clear. She's in the room across the hall, boiling a kettle."

Three more SWARM micro-robots emerged from their hiding places. Hercules the stag beetle crawled from under the desk. Nero the scorpion emerged from behind heavy, patterned curtains. Sabre the tiny mosquito had been absolutely still, attached to the ceiling in one corner of the room.

"We should go after her," he transmitted to the others. "Stick closely to her every movement."

"No, Sirena can monitor what she's doing," said Nero. "It's very important that we remain undetected. Our job here is to guard Dr Smith in case the people who've stolen Whiplash arrive."

"It's lucky those crooks don't know about us," said Hercules. "Nero could crack that code in minutes. They wouldn't need Dr Smith's help."

"Speaking of help…" said Nero. He scuttled across the desk to where Dr Smith had left her tablet covered in calculations. With one of his pincers, he deleted a "3" in the middle of the screen and changed it to a "2".

"There," he said. "The formula works correctly now."

"She's coming back," said Sirena.

The SWARM robots retreated to their hiding places.

Dr Smith came in, sipping from a steaming mug. Sitting down at the desk, she ran a finger along the lines of calculations she'd written.

"Ah!" she said to herself. "It does work. I was right all along." She picked up the pen and went back to work, clicking open a fresh page and scribbling rapidly across it.

Moments later, Sirena's ultra-sensitive antennae picked up movement outside the house.

"Perhaps it's just a visitor," transmitted Hercules.

"I don't think so," said Sirena. "There are … four life forms approaching from the east. That's across the back garden. Ordinary visitors wouldn't come that way."

Dr Smith carried on working. She'd heard nothing outside, and the robots' transmissions were imperceptible to the human ear.

"Let's get out there," said Sabre.

"Wait," said Nero. "We mustn't take action unless we're sure they're hostile. Our orders are clear."

Sirena's antennae waved slowly. The life forms had stopped moving. She was detecting tiny vibrations and sounds. "They're at the back door now," she said. "I think they may be picking the lock."

"That's enough for me," said Sabre. "They're hostile."

He dropped down from the ceiling and headed for the kitchen.

"Attack mode," said Nero. "Prepare to disable intruders."

As they crept through the back door, Bullman

and his men switched on signal jammers sewn into their combat jackets.

Suddenly, the SWARM robots felt a slight smothering sensation.

"What's that weird feeling in my sensors?" said Hercules.

"They're blocking all outgoing transmissions," said Nero. "They must be jamming all signals in case Dr Smith has got a personal alarm system. Sirena, try to alert the human SWARM agents waiting as backup in the village!"

"Too late," said Sirena. "Contact lost."

"We're on our own," said Nero.

"But we are still managing to communicate with each other," said Hercules.

"We're close enough to each other for our high-band frequencies to get through," said Nero.

Suddenly, the study door flew open. Bullman rushed in, followed by Fraser and two others.

Dr Smith swung around, her eyes wide with fright. "What's going on?" she demanded.

Sabre immediately darted across the study. Nero and Hercules paused for a moment, their programming confused by the signal jammers.

Then they also sped towards the intruders.

Sirena had already made a positive identification of both Bullman and Fraser. She fluttered rapidly, taking sensor readings.

Bullman grabbed hold of Dr Smith, one of his arms gripped tightly around her throat. With a sharp cry, she jabbed him hard in the ribs with her elbow. He let go with a yelp of pain. She spun around and punched him across the jaw. He flew back into the nearest bookcase, toppling books on to him.

"Get out my house, the lot of you!" she cried.

The SWARM robots held off for a few seconds, surprised by Dr Smith's fierce response. But the four intruders recovered quickly and overpowered her.

"Contact with HQ lost," said Nero. "Proceed without orders. Calculation of probabilities indicates we should repel the intruders but not disable them. If we can follow them, we can find Whiplash."

"Logged," said the others. "We're live!"

Sabre swooped down on Bullman. The

mosquito loaded shock pellets into his needle-sharp stinger and jabbed through the hair at the back of Bullman's neck.

"OW!" screamed Bullman, jerking as he received a sharp electric shock. "What the—" He swatted madly at the mosquito buzzing around his head.

With a flick of his body, Nero launched himself at Fraser and scuttled up the man's trouser leg.

Fraser yelled, "Something's crawling on me!" just before Nero delivered a series of stings from ankle to knee. Fraser buckled over in pain, smacking at the back of his trousers. Nero emerged at Fraser's belt line and scurried for his neck. Fraser squealed in a high-pitched voice.

Meanwhile, one of the other intruders had trodden on Hercules. The man's boot was sliced apart with a quick movement of Hercules's saw-like claw. The stag beetle's super-tough exoskeleton wasn't even scratched, but the intruder leaped back with a cry of pain.

Dr Smith hadn't spotted the SWARM robots, and she couldn't understand what was happening. She was about to reach for her phone, which had been knocked off the desk, when Bullman reared up in front of her.

His face was red with concentration and pain. Sabre shocked him twice more, once in the back and once on the top of the head, but the stocky, scowling man somehow managed to shrug it off. With a snarl, he grasped Dr Smith by her arms and dragged her out of the study.

"Come on, you lot!" he shouted at the other three. "Let's get out of this fleapit!"

Dr Smith kicked her legs wildly, but Bullman lifted her off the floor and carried her out.

Meanwhile, Sirena was keeping track of the other SWARM robots. Now it was clear that the intruders wouldn't simply be scared off, Sabre was flying close behind Bullman and Nero was on Bullman's shoulder. Both of them quickly slipped into the side pocket of Dr Smith's jacket. Hercules appeared, flying low to the ground, then he swung upwards in a smooth arc and also tucked himself away in that pocket.

"Sirena," signalled Nero, "the three of us will stay with Dr Smith, and find out where she's being taken. We'll report back as soon as we can. Get clear of the jammers and inform SWARM HQ."

"I'm live," said Sirena.

Fraser and the other two kidnappers staggered after Bullman, limping and rubbing their sore limbs.

"Move it!" Bullman shouted as he carted Dr Smith out to their car, which was parked along a dirt track to one side of the house. Dr Smith kicked and cursed angrily all the way.

Sirena hovered high above them all. She kept testing her connection to headquarters, and to the human SWARM agents in the nearby village, but still could not get through. She turned and flew in the opposite direction. With those jammers switched on, she was the only one who could get news to SWARM about what had happened. Just as soon as she was out of range of the interference that was blocking her signals!

As the car sped away into the distance, Sirena found she could finally sense the outside world again. She flew on into the darkness of the night.

"Sirena to SWARM! Sirena to SWARM! Come in, SWARM!"

CHAPTER SEVEN

Hours later, Bullman's car turned off the main road into a secluded lay-by. It slowed to a crawl while he checked that there were no other cars about. With the coast clear, the car revved up and bumped on to a narrow track, which led down to a sloping patch of land. To each side of the muddy track, reed-like grasses grew tall and wild. It was still dark, but the first red streaks of dawn were showing on the horizon.

They were in East London, in an area beside the Thames that had once been a stretch of small factories and industrial units, but was closed down and abandoned years ago. Now, the decaying shells of small office blocks and warehouses rose up out of the grass as far as the eye could see, like dead whales surfacing on a pale green ocean.

The car was long out of sight of the road. Its headlights were switched off. It descended the slope towards what had once been a busy dockside.

On the back seats, Dr Madeleine Smith was squashed between two of her kidnappers. Bullman and Fraser had managed to tie her wrists and her ankles with rope, but nothing stopped her fighting back.

She headbutted the thug to her left and he howled. The one to her right was pressed against the car door. She wriggled down, pulled up her legs and gave Fraser, sitting in the front passenger seat, a hard kick.

"Stop doing that!" whined Fraser. "Bullman, are we nearly there yet?"

"Nearly," said Bullman, concentrating on his driving. He was as keen to get away from Dr Smith's continued onslaught as the rest of them.

SWARM

Still inside the darkness of Dr Smith's pocket were the three SWARM micro-robots.

"Can either of you link to SWARM HQ yet?" signalled Nero.

"No. The kidnappers must still have those signal jammers switched on," said Hercules.

"We should attack again," said Sabre. "Disable the kidnappers and transmit our data back to headquarters."

"No, we wait," said Nero. "Logic says they'll be taking Dr Smith back to whoever is in charge, who will probably be at their hideout. We need to find out more. If we attack now, we may lose that chance."

"Agreed," said Hercules.

"Our motion is slowing. I think the car has stopped," said Sabre.

Bullman parked the car in the entrance to an old warehouse so it wouldn't be visible from the air. The four kidnappers cautiously manoeuvred Dr Smith out of the back seat. She scowled at them, her eyes ablaze with fury.

Hazy daylight was just beginning to filter across the sky. The kidnappers carried Dr Smith across a short patch of grass to what looked like a little hut. It was a squat grey structure, built of concrete. Its entrance had a large metal wheel to seal the door.

Dr Smith was carried, struggling and cursing, into the strange structure and Bullman sealed the entrance behind them. "You can turn off your signal jammers now," he said. "We're inside the bunker."

The SWARM robots felt their sensors suddenly return to action.

"At last. Contacting SWARM HQ!" said Sabre. "Wait. The transmission is bouncing back. We're still cut off."

"Wherever we are now," said Nero, "it must have some sort of shielding of its own."

The kidnappers carried Dr Smith the length of a narrow concrete corridor that sloped sharply downwards. Dim lights shone behind metal cages in the roof. The air felt cold and damp.

"What is this place?" said Dr Smith.

"This?" said Bullman, his voice echoing along the corridor. "This is our base of operations. A place where nobody will ever find us. Or you."

Dr Smith felt a stab of fear and her anger dissolved into nervousness. She stopped struggling, and looked around for some clue as to where she had been taken.

At the same moment, Sirena was back in the laboratory at headquarters. She flew down on to the workbench in front of Simon Turing, landing gently on a large, rectangular shape. At the point where her thin metal legs touched the surface a series of red circles began to spin outwards, like ripples from a stone dropped in water.

"I've finally got the download pads up and running," said Simon to Queen Bee. "It makes retrieving data from the robots much easier."

Queen Bee wasn't in any mood for pleasantries. She turned to Sirena, who was closing up her wings into their standby position, forming a large colourful triangle above her back. "Sirena, you say Nero, Sabre and Hercules are shadowing Dr Smith?"

"Affirmative, Queen Bee," said Sirena, her voice

coming from a speaker set into the workbench. "They're live, but out of contact." She sent her last sensor readings up to the laboratory's 3D display.

Queen Bee and Simon watched Bullman's car vanishing into the night. "No word from them at all?" said Queen Bee. She tried not to let her concern show in her voice.

"Nothing, Queen Bee," said Simon. "Professor Miller is trying to boost our communication systems right now, but no luck so far. They dropped off our detection grid at Dr Smith's house, and since then, nothing."

"So they're totally on their own," said Queen Bee. "This whole operation now rests on how those three agents perform."

"Let's hope they're as good as we think they are," replied Simon.

Queen Bee stood gazing at the 3D display for a moment, lost in thought. She hadn't told anyone that she'd just been on the phone to the Home Secretary again. The Home Secretary had reminded her that SWARM only had a few hours to recover Whiplash before they placed the mission in the hands of MI5 and shut the department down forever. Queen Bee was not about to tell the rest of the team that she had lied to the Home Secretary in order to play for time. She'd claimed that the micro-robots were closing in on the thieves, that SWARM HQ was in full control of the situation, and that the targets would be arrested very soon.

If the robots failed in their mission, not only would SWARM be shut down, but Queen Bee would be in very serious trouble.

She suddenly seemed to snap back to life. "I'll check on how the Professor's doing," she said, and marched out of the laboratory.

"Good morning, Dr Smith. My name is Williams."

Williams smiled down at her. She recoiled slightly. They were in a small, bare room inside the Operation New Age bunker. Dr Smith was seated at a battered wooden table, her ankles tied tightly to the legs of her chair. On the table in front of her were a laptop, a writing pad and a biro. The only light came from a desk lamp poised above the laptop.

"May I call you Madeleine?" said Williams.

Dr Smith glared up at him, trying not to let her terror show. "No, you may not! Whatever you want, I won't cooperate. Who were those scum who dragged me from my home?"

"Just some friends of mine. They're having all their cuts and bruises attended to. You put up quite a fight," said Williams, clearly amused.

"Let me out of here! Please!"

"That's not going to happen," Williams replied.

Dr Smith looked at her grim surroundings. She tried not to feel nervous, but that was easier said than done. "What is this place?" she said.

Williams slowly walked around her. "It was built in the early 1980s," he said, "during the Cold War, when Russia and America were threatening each other with nuclear weapons, and the prospect of a ruined planet was frighteningly close. This is a bunker. A shelter from atomic warfare. Now it's our base of operations. It was designed to keep about fifty people safe from the bomb blasts and radiation. It's got its own air-filtering pumps, everything."

"And I'm supposed to believe that it was just abandoned?" said Dr Smith.

"Along with the industrial complex around it, yes. The businesses went bust. This bunker was supposed to be top secret, even when it was built. It extends underground beneath the River Thames." He pointed up at the concrete roof. "Above where you're sitting are millions of tonnes of water. There's only one way in and out. Put any thought of escape right out of your mind."

Dr Smith felt more nervous than ever now. "You've wasted your time kidnapping me," she said, trying to keep her voice level. "Nobody I know has got any money. You won't get much of a ransom for me!"

"We don't want your money, Dr Smith, we want your mind. The computer in front of you shows details of a coded electronic locking system. Your job is to tell us what that code is. You have everything here you need, I think. Computer, pen, paper, brain."

"I won't do it!"

Williams loomed over the table. The light of

the desk lamp threw twisted shadows across his face. "Aww, you disappoint me," he sighed. "I thought you'd be a sensible girl. Oh well, you'll still be able to work with a broken leg. Or even two broken legs."

"It'll take more than your threats to frighten me!" cried Dr Smith. "I'll never crack that code! I don't care what you want it for, or how much you try to scare me, it's not happening. OK? Do you hear me? Never!"

Williams tutted quietly and shook his head. Then he pulled an envelope from his pocket. "Have I got to resort to this? Huh? Have I?"

He opened the envelope and pulled out a handful of papers. One by one, he dropped them on to the table in front of Dr Smith. There were photos, addresses and phone numbers.

"Here we are, then," said Williams cheerily. "It's amazing what you can find online. We know where your parents live, and your three best friends. We have details of the vet where your lovely dog Sam is recovering from his operation. Do you need more? Do you need me to spell out what will happen if we don't get our code? Ah,

I can see from your face that you understand. Excellent."

Williams gathered up the papers and slipped them back into the envelope. Dr Smith began to tap at the keys of the laptop in front of her. Her face was a battle between steaming anger and terror.

"I'll leave you in peace, then," said Williams. "Someone will be back soon to check on your progress."

The door clicked shut behind him.

CHAPTER EIGHT

Inside Dr Smith's pocket, the three SWARM robots prepared to move out.

"We'll have to blow our cover," said Nero. "I've run the maths on our options and it's our only real choice. We'll have to reveal to Dr Smith that we are robots – she can't escape without us, and we can't recover Whiplash without her."

"Let's go!" said Sabre.

"Don't be so hasty," said Hercules.

"Letting an unauthorized human know about us is strictly against SWARM rules," said Nero. "SWARM is a top-secret organization, and we are the most top-secret part of SWARM. Our programming is very clear on that point."

"Our programming also tells us to think for ourselves," said Sabre. "We're out of contact with SWARM, and we have to make our own decisions. What is more important – keeping our existence secret from Dr Smith or the success of the mission? We can be very clear on that point too."

"Agreed," said Hercules. "Recovering Whiplash must be our first priority."

"We have to be cautious about how we reveal ourselves to Dr Smith," added Nero. "At this moment she is experiencing emotions such as fear and anger."

"Humans are weird," muttered Hercules.

"Agreed," continued Nero, "but we mustn't do anything to make the situation worse. She might panic, or believe we are part of Williams's gang. She might even tell Williams about us, and then SWARM itself would be at risk."

"We should locate Whiplash first," said Hercules, "and only show ourselves once we've gathered whatever information we can."

"Should we leave her working on the code?" said Sabre. "Is that wise?"

"Our programming tells me that complicated tasks help focus a human's thoughts," said Nero. "Working on the code will calm her down. By the time we've gathered data, she should be in a more logical frame of mind. Then we won't scare her. Besides, robots are much more efficient than humans. I'm sure it would take me only a few minutes to crack the code, but even Dr Smith will probably take hours."

The three robots carefully emerged from their hiding place and crawled away down the back of the chair. Dr Smith was concentrating on the computer screen in front of her and jotting notes on the writing pad. She glanced up briefly, distracted by a faint buzz, but quickly returned to her code-breaking.

The robots easily made it under the door and out into the narrow corridor beyond. To the left, their scans revealed the bunker's main control room, where the gang was preparing Phase One of Operation New Age. To the right, they could detect voices coming from one of the rooms about ten metres away.

"Sabre, you gather visuals," said Nero. "Photograph and scan everything going on in this bunker. I'll get into their computers. Hercules, cut access holes wherever possible, in case we need a rapid escape route, and monitor whoever goes near Dr Smith."

"We're live," said Sabre and Hercules. Sabre took to the air and sped away. Nero scuttled rapidly into the control room, while Hercules flew up to an electrical box bolted to a nearby wall, cut a small hole in it and crawled inside.

They transmitted streams of data to each other as they progressed. "Eye cameras at enhanced level," said Sabre. "Images of all gang members obtained. Watching activity."

Nero kept to the shadows at the edge of the large control room, skirting around the equipment until he found a blank metal plate on the back of a PC. Using a screwdriver attachment inside one of his claws, he quickly undid the plate and squeezed inside. He tested the computer's processors until he found a suitable patch of circuitry. Then a tiny fibre-optic probe extended from his claw and clamped on, linking him to the gang's computer network.

"Can you send a message?" said Sabre.

"Negative," said Nero. "All communication with the outside world is routed through Williams's own smartphone. I can't bypass that without tripping several automatic alarms. However, I can read every byte of data that's gone through here since it was first switched on."

Hercules was snipping and chewing his way through various air vents, and pipes designed for electrical cables. "Give me the full layout of the bunker, Nero," he said. "That way I can check that I won't cut through any cable I shouldn't."

"Accessing," said Nero. The probe searched the computer's hard drives. "I've got it," said Nero. "Detailed drawings of the whole place."

"Received," said Hercules.

"Wait," said Nero. "I've found a lot more in here... Hang on... Accessing... Accessing..."

Meanwhile, Hercules emerged from a neatly cut hole in a metal heating duct. He found himself in the long concrete corridor that led away from the bunker's entrance.

The large metal wheel in the centre of the door was turning.

"Someone's coming in!" said Hercules.

"You might be able to slip past them." transmitted Sabre. "If you leave the bunker, you can contact HQ!"

The bunker's entrance swung open. Hercules instantly flicked his wings to full stretch and took off. Whereas Sabre, and Chopper the dragonfly, were built for agility and would have reached the entrance in seconds, Hercules was designed for heavier work, and his top speed was much lower. He was eighteen metres away from freedom…

A figure stepped through the entrance into the sinister gloom of the corridor.

Fifteen metres…

The figure turned and took hold of the metal locking wheel.

Ten metres…

The heavy metal door was swung back.

Seven metres…

The door bumped shut, the wheel was turned and the bunker was sealed up once more. Hercules swerved in mid-air and landed on the wall above the entrance.

"Attempt failed," he transmitted to the others. "The door wasn't open long enough. I got a brief look at our visitor, though."

He sent his sensor readings to the others. They pieced together a photograph that was too blurry to give a positive identification.

"I'll intercept him," said Sabre. "I can see he's entering the control room now." With a sharp buzz, Sabre skimmed along the ceiling.

Nero, still plugged into the computer system, had accessed a treasure trove of documents, emails, phone calls and technical data. "The information I've tapped into tells us almost all we need to know," he said. "To begin with, it seems this bunker is safe from the effects of Whiplash. It's built using thick concrete reinforced with layers of lead and other metals. That's why our signals can't get through."

"I have an idea," said Hercules. "I could cut through the wall of the bunker, at a point close to the entrance. It would take a while, and it would use up most of my processing capactiy, but if I could tunnel through to the outside, our contact problem would be solved."

"Logged," said Nero. "Begin at once."

Hercules set his pincers to emit tiny ultra-sonic vibrations, far too high for human ears to hear. He focused them on to a single spot in the wall ahead, hitting the concrete with just enough energy to loosen its molecules and allow Hercules's pincers to dig in. Slowly but surely he chewed his way into the wall.

Meanwhile, Nero's processor was in overdrive, sorting and assembling the details of Operation New Age from the mass of information.

"It appears that we were correct. Williams's gang have had a mole inside Techna-Stik all along," he said. "They've been getting information about Whiplash from someone they know only as the Insider. This person has visited the bunker several times over the past few days."

"Logic would suggest that this Insider is the newcomer who's just entered the control room," said Sabre. "Gathering detailed visuals now." He flew level with the newcomer's face, and transmitted an image to the others.

Within seconds the robots had a swift and

definite ID. Nero cross-checked against the mission data Simon Turing had uploaded. There was no doubt.

"The Insider is Mr Haynes, Techna-Stik's UK Operations Director," said Nero.

"Why would the boss of the company that created Whiplash help other people to steal it?"

"Listen to this," said Nero. "Williams has been lying to his gang. They think they're engaged in a plan codenamed Operation New Age. Phase One is genuine – it involves firing Whiplash to cause havoc across southern England. But Phase Two is a complete fantasy. I've traced and reconstructed a call between Williams and the Insider, or rather Mr Haynes, two hours seventeen minutes ago. Listen."

There was a crackle of static on the robots' communication circuit, then they heard…

Williams: It's me. How are preparations going?

Haynes: Fine. The Gylbut Gadgets factory is ready to start producing Whiplash shielding as soon as we need it. The sooner the better, I've got the banks hounding me for money. They're hounding Oliphant too. He's going to give in and let them take everything he owns but he's not dragging me down with him!

Williams: That's your problem. Me, I'm having trouble not laughing out loud.

Haynes: What do you mean?

Williams: This bunch of dimwits here. The closer we get to Phase One the more they're getting like a bunch of kiddies on Christmas Eve. Pathetic.

Haynes: Don't underestimate them. They're badly misguided, but they're not stupid. Are you sure we'll be able to get away?

Williams: Of course, stop fussing. I told you, once Whiplash is fired, they'll all be in party mode. I'll pocket the weapon, then you and I can slip away. They have no idea who we really are and they'll all be wanted by the cops for terrorism.

Haynes: All I'm saying is, have we covered every angle?

Williams: I have. Are you coming in soon?

Haynes: Yes, I'll be at the bunker in a couple of hours. I'm just going to stop off at home and put all my electronics in one of the new Gylbut Gadgets protector boxes. Don't want my TVs ruined when Whiplash goes off.

Williams: OK.

There was another crackle of static and the recording ended.

"Why fire Whiplash and walk away?" said Sabre. "What is Mr Haynes's connection to Gylbut Gadgets? Aren't they Techna-Stik's main business rival? Why do both Haynes and Oliphant owe the bank a lot of money?"

"I'm continuing to sort and assemble data," said Nero. "We need more answers."

"Have you found Whiplash itself?" said Sabre.

"Almost," said Nero. "It's location is masked

by layers of security… Accessing… Accessing…"

"If Williams is also using a fake identity," said Sabre, "then who is he really?"

Nero was too busy to answer. "Got it! Whiplash is plugged into a circuit board beneath the workstation closest to the corridor."

Hercules had tunnelled through nearly two metres of heavily reinforced concrete and he was still working. Now he'd come up against the lead-lined outer shell of the bunker. The plans sent to him by Nero told him that this shell was made of thick metal sheets and would be extremely difficult to break through. His own sensors readings were telling him the same thing.

He powered up the plasma-cutting torches at the tips of his pincers. They began to glow white-hot. His energy cells were starting to send "Low" signals to his CPU but he ignored the warnings. With ultra-sonic vibrations set to maximum and his pincers showering the tiny tunnel with molten metal sparks, he moved slowly forward.

Meanwhile, Nero and Sabre were moving their plans forward. "Whiplash located in the main control room, docked in the first computer on the left. I can remove the weapon from its casing," he said, "but getting it out of the bunker may be a problem. I have more than enough strength to carry it, but it would be almost impossible to transport without being seen. Hercules, could you fly it out?"

"I've got my pincers full at the moment," said Hercules.

"Then it's time to free Dr Smith," said Sabre.

"Agreed," said Nero.

The two of them hurried back to the room where Dr Smith was being held captive, Nero skittering along in the shadows, Sabre humming close to the ceiling.

As they approached the room, they were just in time to see Williams march in. "Well?" he demanded.

Dr Smith, her ankles still securely tied to the chair, was now much more calm. "Done," she declared. "Rather easy, actually."

With a grin, Williams looked at the screen of

the laptop. After a long string of calculations and formulae, a line read:

CALCULATION VERIFIED: ⱻ4ᴍF04ᴎ90414ᴊF

Williams scooped up the laptop and snapped it shut. "Thank you," he smiled. "We'll enter this code into our system immediately. The countdown can begin."

"Countdown?" said Dr Smith. "The countdown to what?"

"None of your business," sneered Williams. "Your usefulness has ended."

"Then you can let me go!" yelled Dr Smith. "Immediately! I've done what you asked, now untie me!"

Williams stood over her. His shadow fell across her face. "No," he said quietly. "Sorry about that. We can't have you blabbing to the police, can we? You're not leaving here, ever."

"You can't do this!" Dr Smith cried. "I demand you let me go!"

Williams spoke in a low growl. "Think yourself lucky I don't have you killed right now." He marched out of the room.

Dr Smith let out an angry yell and began to tug uselessly at the ropes around her legs.

"Humans are more efficient than I thought," said Nero.

"At least, that one is," said Sabre.

"We'll have to act quickly," said Nero. "Before Williams and the gang fire Whiplash."

CHAPTER NINE

00:00:05

"Countdown set at five minutes! Mark! Four minutes fifty-nine seconds … fifty-eight seconds … fifty-seven…" The metallic voice of the computer system echoed throughout the bunker.

The gang members began to chatter with excitement. Bullman sat back on the old leather sofa in the corner of the control room, his face alight. Fraser breathed a sigh of relief and continued tapping at the keyboard of his PC. Williams and the Insider were huddled over the screen where they'd just entered Whiplash's code.

"Aren't you nervous?" whispered Haynes.

"What for?" whispered Williams. "I'm staying right here by this computer. As soon as Whiplash detonates, I open the hatch at the back down there, unplug it, pocket it and we're out of here."

"What if Bullman or one of the others asks where we're going?"

"What, we can't make up a reason to pop outside? Get a grip. Nothing can go wrong."

The countdown continued. "Four minutes thirty-four seconds ... thirty-three ... thirty-two..."

Meanwhile, Nero and Sabre had positioned themselves beneath Dr Smith's chair. She had given up struggling to loosen the ropes.

"Switch external speakers on," transmitted Nero.

"On and set at maximum," sent Sabre. "Let's hope she has good hearing, for a human."

Together they crawled up on to the table and came to a stop directly in front of Dr Smith. At first, she was too distracted to notice them.

Nero's voice came out of a tiny oval shape built into his thorax. To a human's ears it sounded faint and distant. "Dr Madeleine Smith," he said. "Please do not be afraid. We are here to help you."

Dr Smith suddenly flicked her head left and right, wondering where the strange voice had come from. Then she noticed a scorpion and a mosquito standing still as statues on the table.

She let out a sharp yelp and tried to push back her chair. "S-Scorpion!" she squealed. "They're going to kill me with a scorpion!"

"My name is Nero," came the tiny voice. "This is my co-agent, Sabre. We are not organic, we are micro-robots, and we're here to help you. Please do not be afraid."

"Robots?" she said. "I must be going mad. I'm letting the situation get the better of me."

"We assure you, this is no trick," said Sabre.

"Where did you come from?" asked Dr Smith, staring uncertainly at them.

"We're members of a secret organization," said Sabre. "We are on a mission to recover a dangerous weapon called Whiplash. The countdown you can hear will end in the weapon being fired. It emits a massive electro-magnetic pulse. The effects will be devastating."

Dr Smith nodded. "We've got to get out of here! My father has a heart pacemaker. An EMP will kill him instantly!"

"The robots at SWARM HQ will also die if Whiplash fires," said Sabre.

Nero was already scuttling down to the ropes around Dr Smith's ankles. Extending his pincers, he began to cut her loose.

"Not quite as quick as Hercules," he said, "but still efficient."

"Hercules is a stag beetle," said Sabre.

"Yes," muttered Dr Smith, nervously watching Nero slice into the ropes. "Of course he is."

Overhead, the computer's countdown moved closer to disaster. "Three minutes nineteen seconds to firing ... three minutes eighteen ... seventeen..."

The ropes suddenly fell slack.

"Now, Dr Smith, it's time to retrieve the weapon and get out of here," said Nero.

Dr Smith rubbed at her ankles and stood up.

Nero hopped on to the shoulder of her jacket, and Sabre buzzed along beside her. The mosquito peeped out into the corridor.

"I can't see anyone," she breathed.

"We must create a diversion," said Nero. "The control room is full of humans but we have to get in there to recover Whiplash."

"How?" said Dr Smith.

Nero consulted the plans of the bunker and came up with an idea in less than a millionth of a second. "Please move back along the corridor. Seven metres behind you, on the wall, is a metal panel."

Checking to make sure nobody was coming, Dr Smith tiptoed to the panel and opened it. The panel swung down. Inside was a series of dials, like the pressure gauges on an old-fashioned steam engine. Beneath them was a line of switches and buttons.

"The bunker is partially built beneath the River Thames," explained Nero. "This panel opens a set of gates holding the water back. It was a last-resort feature of the bunker, in case of the enemy gaining entry."

"What?" gasped Dr Smith. "You're going to flood this place? That's crazy! You've got to be joking."

"I don't joke," said Nero. "We'll allow water to enter slowly. There's only one exit. Everyone will have to evacuate the bunker. If we don't manage to retrieve Whiplash in time, then Sabre and I can stay behind to get it. We can operate underwater for a short time."

"Two minutes twenty-four seconds..." the countdown reverberated along the corridor. "Twenty-three seconds ... twenty-two..."

"OK, what do I do?" asked Dr Smith, taking a deep breath. "No, wait, I can guess. I need to pull this lever out, yes?"

"Correct," said Nero, "pull and turn to the right. It needs a human's strength. That unlocks the bolts holding the gates in place."

"Then blow the bolts using this big red button?"

"Correct," said Nero. "Have you been studying the bunker's systems?"

"No," said Dr Smith, "I've just seen a lot of action films." Without another word, she grasped hold of the small hand lever in front of her and pulled hard. It didn't budge. After a few seconds of effort, she let go with a gasp and flexed her fingers. "I think it's rusted," she muttered.

"Two minutes fourteen seconds..." boomed the countdown. "Thirteen seconds..."

"I'll give it another go," said Dr Smith. She breathed in deeply and took hold of the lever again. Then she clenched her teeth and heaved. Still it didn't move.

Suddenly, Sabre swung around in mid-air. "Movement detected."

Fraser the computer hacker appeared at the other end of the corridor. For a split second, he remained frozen in surprise, staring directly at Dr Smith. Dr Smith stared back, one hand on the lever.

Fraser dropped the clipboard he was carrying and fled back to the control room. "Hey! Stop!" he yelled. "The prisoner's escaping!"

"Uh-oh," said Dr Smith.

"Pull the lever quickly," said Nero. "Our chances of success have now reduced by approximately half."

Voices were raised inside the control room.

Several gang members, including Bullman, spilled out into the corridor and raced to intercept Dr Smith.

"Attack mode," said Sabre. "Electro-sting powered up."

The lever in the wall began to move, very slowly. The gang members closed in. Sabre, with his eye cameras keeping track of all of them, darted left and right.

"Yee-ooww!" screamed the nearest gang member, as Sabre swooped to deliver a painful shock to the end of his nose. The man fell back, his hands to his face.

Sabre whipped to the opposite side of the corridor. A second jab sent another man reeling, this time clutching his shoulder.

Bullman stormed ahead.

Sabre knew that Bullman wouldn't be stopped by an electric sting. He switched his injector to stun pellets. He had three of them left.

The lever moved slowly, slowly. Dr Smith used every bit of strength she had.

"One minute thirty-four seconds ... thirty-three..."

Bullman charged at Dr Smith with a roar. She yelped with fright and Sabre swiftly stung him in the neck with a freezer stun pellet.

Bullman staggered. For a moment, his eyes rolled and he sagged at the shoulders. Then he grunted loudly, shook himself and reared up. Sabre delivered a second pellet, behind Bullman's ear.

The man tottered. His eyes tried to focus... What was that? A fly? His face curled into a grimace and he raised his fists. Sabre stung him one more time.

Bullman rocked on his heels, his face suddenly blank. Then he crashed backwards on to the floor, completely senseless.

With Bullman down, Dr Smith turned back to the lever and continued to twist.

At last the lever clicked into place. Dr Smith smacked the red button in the centre of the wall panel.

"One minute to firing … fifty-nine seconds … fifty-eight…"

Water began to gush from a grille close to floor level.

Dr Smith leaped back. "Wow, that's cold!" she gasped.

The water spread rapidly across the floor, turning the dusty concrete the colour of cold tea. A loud, warbling alarm began to sound but the countdown continued. A rancid smell rose off the water as it hissed and flowed.

In the control room, there was panic. A thin sheet of water was already seeping past the doorway.

"Seal the door!" cried Fraser. "Seal the door! Keep the water out!"

"Don't be a fool!" barked Williams. "We'll be trapped in here! Where's Bullman? Get that water shut off! Now!"

Out in the corridor, Nero was sabotaging the panel in the wall. Sparks flew around him as he snipped at the panel's controls. "There," he said. "The grille is locked in the open position. They can't turn the water off." He hopped back on to Dr Smith's shoulder. "Now we head for the control room."

"Forty seconds to firing … thirty-nine … thirty-eight…"

Williams was in a fury, yelling at the gang members to remain at their stations. Few of them were taking any notice of him. Most were either retreating from the flood or wading along the corridor. Fraser and another man were dragging the unconscious Bullman towards the bunker's exit. The water was almost ankle-deep now, and rising fast.

"What do we do?" cried Haynes. "Williams! What do we do?"

"The countdown is still going," cried Williams, above the rushing of the flood and the bleating of the alarm siren. "Just over half a minute left. The water won't get high enough to short the computers in that time. Whiplash will still fire!"

"I'm getting out now!" cried Haynes.

"Stay where you are, you snivelling coward!" yelled Williams. "There'll be time to get the weapon and make it outside!"

"Twenty-seven seconds … twenty-six…"

The gang members were crowding along the corridor, making for the exit.

Dr Smith appeared at the entrance to the control room.

Williams swung round and glared at her. "Look what you've done, you witch!" he screeched.

Nero, clinging to her collar, spoke close to her ear. "There's a hatch near your left knee, with a black flip-up catch. Whiplash is behind that."

Williams suddenly pulled a gun from a holster hidden under his shirt, a snub-barrelled pistol. He levelled it at Dr Smith. "I should have killed you earlier!"

"Twenty seconds to firing … nineteen…"

"I'm getting out!" cried Haynes. "No amount of money is worth this!" He turned to leave, making waves in the rising water as he walked.

"Haynes!" bellowed Williams, turning to face the other man. "Stay where you are! I order you to stop!"

Haynes didn't answer. He waded away as fast as he could.

With a fierce glint of hatred in his eyes, Williams raised the gun and fired.

Haynes dropped face-first into the water.

"Seventeen … sixteen…"

Williams swung the gun back to aim at Dr Smith. She tightened her hands into fists and stared right back at him.

In Nero's lightning-fast brain, millions of sensor readings told him Williams was pulling the trigger of the gun almost before Williams himself was aware of it. He calculated the precise path the bullet would take, its speed and impact point.

The scorpion sprung into the air as Williams fired. He spun, at full stretch, and the bullet flashed into range. The tip of Nero's tail, reaching out as far as it could go, brushed the bullet as it passed. The bullet's path was deflected, only by a millimetre but just enough to send it skimming past the edge of Dr Smith's hair. It smacked into the wall, a shower of concrete bursting behind it.

"Sabre," said Nero. "Attack mode."

"I'm live," said Sabre.

Sabre first stung Williams on the back of his hand. He dropped the gun with a yell of pain and Sabre stung again, on his chin. Williams staggered. Sabre continued stinging until Williams was at the other end of the room, swatting wildly all around himself.

"Ow! Aaargh!"

"Ten seconds … nine…"

Williams was no longer a threat, but the Whiplash countdown continued.

Dr Smith was standing, still in shock.

Nero got as close to her ear as he could. "Dr Smith, we've got to stop Whiplash."

Dr Smith snapped back to the urgency of the situation. She knelt and fumbled with the catch at the back of the computer where the small device was docked. Freezing water rushed around her waist.

"Eight … seven…"

The hatch dropped down. Inside was a large circuit board with a whole range of chips and devices attached. "Which is it? Which is it?"

"The blue one," said Nero calmly.

Dr Smith reached for it and pulled – but the weapon was held tightly in the port.

"Six … five…"

"I can't free it!"

Nero scuttled along her arm and into the machine.

"Four…"

Nero pushed at the weapon with a pincer. One of Whiplash's delicate connector pins was bent double and wedged into place.

"Three..."

Nero knocked it sharply with both pincers. Whiplash popped free and Dr Smith snatched it up.

The whole control room seemed to power down. Displays began to flicker and go blank. They'd done it!

But the alarm continued to wail and the water was steadily rising.

With Nero at her shoulder, and Sabre flying overhead, Dr Smith waded out into the corridor and followed the long slope leading up to the bunker's entrance. The gang members were gathered there, yelling at Fraser to hurry up. Fraser was at the front of the group, turning the metal wheel to open the door.

At last, with a hiss, it swung open and daylight

shone in. Cool fresh air rushed around them. Behind Dr Smith, the flood swirled and crawled up the slope.

The gang pushed and barged their way outside. But their cries of relief quickly turned to despair as they saw the wide ring of armed police officers waiting for them.

Dr Smith staggered over to a sparse patch of grass and sat down. Suddenly, a stag beetle landed close to her feet. A scorpion and a mosquito joined it.

"What kept you?" asked Hercules. "I sent an emergency signal to SWARM fifteen minutes ago. Did it take you longer than expected to recover Whiplash?"

"You could say that," replied Sabre. "What's happened to Williams?" he added, his sensors scanning the area. Water was beginning to lap around the door they'd just emerged from. The bunker was now completed flooded.

Dr Smith felt a hand placed gently on her shoulder. She looked up to see SWARM's human agents, Agent J and Agent K.

"Dr Smith?" said Agent J.

Agent K helped Dr Smith to her feet. "I think this is for you," said Dr Smith, handing Whiplash over to Agent J. "All this trouble over such a small thing."

Agent J beckoned to one of the nearby police officers.

"Yes, sir?" said the officer.

"This is Dr Madeleine Smith," said Agent J. "She'll be taking full credit for foiling the plot."

"Of course, sir. This way, miss."

It wasn't until the officer had led her a few metres away that Dr Smith realized what Agent J had said. "Full credit? No, no, it wasn't my idea to let in the river..."

She turned to speak to Agent J, but there was no sign of him, or Agent K, or any kind of robotic insects. She frowned and shook her head, as she was led to a waiting car.

CHAPTER TEN

"You're sure she won't talk about us?" said Professor Miller. "This was a serious breach of security."

"Dr Smith is a very intelligent person, with an important job," said Queen Bee. "We can trust her to know that claiming she was helped by robotic insects is probably not the sensible option."

Professor Miller nodded. "Yes, I see your point."

They arrived at the laboratory, deep inside SWARM headquarters.

Alfred Berners was debriefing the micro-robots before putting them offline.

"Well done, everyone," said Queen Bee. "Our first full mission has been a success."

The lab's communicator bleeped, and Queen Bee pressed "Accept Call" on the large touchscreen fixed to the wall. The faces of the Home Secretary and the head of MI5 appeared.

"The Prime Minister has asked me to express his gratitude," said the Home Secretary.

"I take it SWARM meets with official approval, then?" said Queen Bee.

"I still don't understand why Williams and Haynes were planning to fire Whiplash and then do nothing," said the Home Secretary.

"It's all down to money," said Queen Bee. "Greed. Once Whiplash had been fired, the whole world would be living in fear of a repeat disaster. With the weapon out of our hands, every electronic item on Earth would need protection from it. Gylbut Gadgets were ready and waiting to make that protection, in the form of their own special shielding. It seems that Williams himself invented the shielding. He held all the patents. Haynes, it turns out, was secretly the owner of Gylbut Gadgets."

"He owned the main business rival of the company he worked for?" said the Home Secretary.

"That's right," said Queen Bee. "He and the Head of Projects at Techna-Stik, Marcus Oliphant, had run up enormous debts. They were fed up with seeing Techna-Stik make money from their ideas, so they financed a number of projects themselves but lost every penny. They were desperately looking for a way out. Haynes had bought Gylbut Gadgets in secret, without Oliphant's knowledge, hoping to find his fortune and pay off his half of the debt that way."

"Leaving Oliphant to sink or swim, I suppose," said the Home Secretary. "So Oliphant didn't know about Operation New Age, or Haynes's link to Gylbut Gadgets?"

"No, he had no idea. Haynes was only concerned about himself. When Williams turned up at Gylbut Gadgets with the idea for EMP shielding, Haynes saw that it fitted perfectly with Techna-Stik's latest development, Whiplash, so Haynes and Williams cooked up the whole Operation New Age plan together."

"The police recovered Haynes's body, I understand?" said the Home Secretary.

"Yes," said Queen Bee, "but not Williams's. His corpse might have been washed out into the Thames when the bunker was drained, but we can't be sure. His true identity is still a complete mystery too." Queen Bee paused, and smiled. "But, of course, tracing who he really was is MI5's job."

The head of MI5 looked daggers at her.

"It seems SWARM has proved its worth," said the Home Secretary.

The communicator screen blinked out. Queen Bee turned to the robots. "We're here to stay," she said.

"Logged, Queen Bee," replied the SWARM team in unison.

At that moment, Simon Turing hurried in. He paused for a moment to catch his breath, then handed Queen Bee a sheet of paper.

"I think you need to see this," he gasped. "It's just come in. If what it says is true, we could be in for big trouble."

"Here we go again," said Hercules.

COMING SOON!

SWARM suspect that a scientist at the
country's top research laboratory has gone
rogue. They uncover a sinister underworld and a
deadly poison that is about to be unleashed.
Can SWARM foil the scientist's evil plan
before the world is changed forever?

Turn the page to read an extract...

CHAPTER ONE

London. 3 September, 3 a.m.

From above, the lights of the city looked like a concentrated cluster of stars. Towards the west, where the cluster began to thin out, the street lights glowed a hazy yellow along the main road. Even in the early hours of the morning, a few cars sped along. Their tyres hissed against the road, damp and shining from a recent shower of rain.

Set back from the road was a large, rectangular

building. It was plain and grey – just like the other factories and office blocks in the area. But this building was surrounded by a high fence.

The fence looked like it was made from ordinary steel, but it was actually constructed from the latest in smart materials, designed to identify even the slightest touch. Alarms would trigger if anyone tried to climb or cut it. At a gate close to the building's main entrance, a security guard sipped a mug of tea in his brightly lit cabin. Across the gate was a swirly silver logo and the words:

SMITH-NEUTALL BIO LABS LTD.
NO UNAUTHORIZED ENTRY.
NO ADMITTANCE WITHOUT BIOMETRIC ID.
TRESPASSERS WILL BE PROSECUTED.

High above, a dragonfly zipped over the gate and headed for the building. Held in its thin legs, was a scorpion. Close behind the dragonfly came a butterfly, carrying a curled-up centipede, then a stag beetle and a tiny buzzing mosquito. Meanwhile, a small spider had shot a line of web at the guard's hut, and was swinging in a wide arc up and over the fence, carried along on the chilly night breeze.

The sight of seven insects making their way towards a heavily guarded building would have been strange enough at the best of times. However, the truth about them was even more strange. All seven were miniature robots, each one an agent of the top-secret security organization SWARM, otherwise known as the Department of Micro-robotic Intelligence. The dragonfly, its iridescent wings shimmering in the glow from the street lights, was code-named Chopper. The scorpion he was carrying was called Nero. Sabre the mosquito and Hercules the stag beetle took up the rear, monitoring for signs that the robots had been followed or detected.

"We'll enter through the exhaust vents on the roof." Chopper's voice registered in the computer brains of his companions.

"Do you have a tight hold on me?" said the coiled centipede. His code name was Morph.

"Don't worry," said the butterfly, Sirena. "I've got you. We're nearly there."

The spider stayed silent. She usually did.

Her code name was Widow, and the micro-fibre threads she spun were stronger than steel. She zipped up on to the flat roof of the building ahead of the others.

Chopper and Sirena landed beside a large metal vent which ended in a flat grille, and Nero and Morph scuttled free. Sabre and Hercules maintained surveillance.

Chopper examined the closed grille using his night vision.

"Entrance blocked," he said. "Morph, bottom left corner shows a gap of 0.8 millimetres."

"Logged," replied Morph. The centipede scurried over. The flexible, gelatinous material of his body allowed him to squeeze through the tiny gap. Inside, he reformed into his normal shape. He found the mechanism and opened the grille, gripping it tightly with his tail. The others quickly entered and Morph let it close behind them.

"Our target could be anywhere in this building," said Chopper. "Mission priority is to locate any high-security storage bays and search them. The target is likely to be small and well hidden. Morph, take over surveillance, watch for movement up here. We must make sure that our exit route is clear. The rest of you, follow me."

Six miniature robots made their way along the ventilation pipe. They met a succession of mesh filters – Hercules the stag beetle cut each one using his serrated claw. After descending for several metres, they entered a high-tech chemistry lab.

The only light came from the distant street lamps visible through the broad, bullet-proof windows. Within the room, LEDs blinked red and green on various pieces of equipment. Plastic biohazard suits were dangling on hooks beside signs:

**"STAY ALERT!
CARELESSNESS KILLS!"**

**"CONTAMINATION DANGER:
ENSURE YOU HAVE AN ALL-CLEAN
CONFIRMED ON ENTERING
AND LEAVING."**

Chopper sent a coded transmission back to SWARM headquarters. "Hive 1 to SWARM."

SWARM's human leader, Beatrice Maynard, code-named Queen Bee, replied instantly.

"I hear you, Chopper, go ahead."

"We're in, Queen Bee," said Chopper. "Operation commencing."

"Begin recording," said Queen Bee. "And be careful."

"Logged, Queen Bee," said Chopper. He scanned the room. Data and images appeared back at HQ on the monitors in front of Queen Bee.

"The target's not here," said Sirena, whose antennae contained SWARM's most sensitive environmental data-gathering systems. "They run tests and experiments in this lab, but there's no secure storage."

"Hack into their computer system, see what you can find," said Chopper.

"Logged," said Sirena. She fluttered to the nearest PC.

Nero hurried over to the laboratory's airtight metal door to unlock it and gain them access to the rest of the building. Tiny probes flicked out from his pincers. They burrowed into a keycode panel. Seconds later, the panel bleeped and the door clunked as it unlocked and opened.

The robots moved out into the corridor beyond. Nero resealed the lab behind them.

"Human twelve metres south," said Chopper.

The robots kept to the shadows. A security guard wandered past the end of the corridor, whistling quietly to himself. Motion-sensitive lights in the walls blinked on as he approached, and off as he went on his way.

"We're too small to set those off," said Chopper.

"But not so small that we can ignore the laser grid," said Hercules.

Halfway down the corridor, a thin red line of light circled walls, ceiling and floor. The beams emitted from it were invisible to humans, but the robots saw them as a flat, moving grid. Each laser beam was powerful enough to slice through them instantly.

"This grid guards the lab," said Chopper. "There are probably more outside other restricted areas."

They watched the grid shifting back and forth for a moment. No human could have calculated a way through it, but within seconds the robots began to dart and jump. They timed their movements precisely, twisting in mid-air to avoid the beams, and landed safely on the other side.

Slowly, they made their way around the building, working downwards from floor to floor. Between them, they recorded every detail of the place.

Nero made a thorough scan of electrical systems. "I'm getting readings of high power usage in the basement," said Nero. "I suspect the bio-storage for holding live viruses and other dangerous substances is down there."

A laser grid outside the basement entrance confirmed that there was something important in there. The robots scuttled and darted past the grid, avoiding the powerful lasers once more.

"Coded alarm system detected in vault door," said Chopper. "Hercules, bypass defences."

The beetle's dark carbon-fibre body would have been invisible to the human eye in the gloom. He scurried up the wall and cut into a small hatch above the basement's entrance. The others swiftly followed him. They crawled into a pipe used for running cables, and moved along it until they reached the room itself.

The vault they looked out on to was low and narrow. Walls, floor and ceiling were all polished metal. At the back was a large glass case labelled with a sign:

The case was filled with rows of coloured bottles and cylinders.

"Nero," said Chopper, "cut a tiny hole in the glass, on the side of the case where it won't be noticed. Sabre, go inside and confirm the target."

"Wait!" said Nero. "I can detect electrical activity in the floor. The area between us and the glass case is sensitive to touch. If it's triggered, the alarm will go off."

"We were small enough not to activate the corridor lights," said Chopper.

"This is different," said Nero. "I'm picking up readings from pressure pads all over the room. If even one of us lands on any connected surface, the alarm will trip. We're very slightly heavier than real insects. The difference is tiny, but it's enough."

"Is the glass case itself wired up?" said Chopper.

"Scanning," said Nero. "No, it isn't."

Widow scuttled forward. Taking careful aim, she fired a thread at the glass case, which stuck neatly at its exact centre.

"A zip line," she said quietly.

Hanging beneath the line by his pincers, Nero slid across to the case. The grippers in his feet engaged with the vertical glass and held him firmly in place. He scuttled around to the side of the case, a miniaturized cutter emerging from a tiny hatch in one pincer, a small suction cup from the other.

He cut a circle in the glass with the cutter, and pulled it free using the suction cup. Then he hurried back along Widow's thread, dangling by his legs.

Sabre buzzed across to the case, keeping well clear of the metal surfaces all around him.

Folding back his mechanical wings, he wriggled through the hole.

"Anything?" transmitted Chopper.

Sabre's needle-like proboscis jutted forward from his mechanical mouthparts. One by one he directed wireless high-frequency probes towards the many glass bottles and Petri dishes around him. "There are various things here. Some of these dishes contain live cell cultures of bacteria, viruses, or other disease pathogens. Some are simply toxic to organic life."

He crawled around the different bottles, each of them covered in printed and handwritten labels, his proboscis scanning and analysing. At last, he approached a small glass phial, set apart from the others. It contained a red liquid which emitted a slight glow. Unlike the others in the case, this container was not marked in any way.

"I've found it," he said.

Chopper signalled SWARM headquarters. "Target located, Queen Bee,"

"Good work," said the voice of Queen Bee. "Sabre, what's your analysis?"

Sabre's sensors processed the data he'd

gathered. "It's a mixture of extracted DNA, viral organisms and poisonous chemicals. It's molecular structure suggests that it affects mammals, birds and fish, some insect species and some reptiles. It kills almost instantly, either by contact or inhalation. There's more information to be retrieved from this data, I'm transmitting it all to you now."

Nero's advanced CPU ran through the necessary calculations in less than a millisecond. "If our analysis so far is correct," he said, "this substance is the most dangerous ever created. An adult human would be dead if exposed to no more than two nanolitres of it. That phial contains 4.93 millilitres. That's enough to kill thirty-eight million people."

There was silence on the line to SWARM headquarters. At last, Queen Bee said "So the information we intercepted last week is correct. But we still don't know if that phial is the only sample of the poison. Or how and why it was made."

"Should we remove this phial?" said Chopper.

"Should we destroy it?" said Nero.

"Negative," said Queen Bee. "Destroying it might make me feel a little safer, but since we don't know if this is all that exists, or whether more can be made easily, that might be a pointless move. We're working on the theory that this is the creation of a single, rogue scientist. However, we have yet to prove that theory. It might be part of a larger project. Removing the phial would alert whoever knows about it to the fact that we'd paid their lab a visit."

"Should I take a small amount of it for further study?" asked Sabre.

"Absolutely not," said Queen Bee. "We can't risk even an atom of that stuff getting loose. No, leave it where it is for now, safely locked away. You've accomplished your mission, and located it. We'll proceed with our original plan: Widow, you stay in the building and shadow the man we suspect. The rest, return to HQ. Good work, all of you."

**Read *PROJECT VENOM*
to find out what happens next!**

SIMON CHESHIRE

Simon is the award-winning author of the *Saxby Smart* and *Jeremy Brown* series. Simon's ultimate dream is to go the moon, but in the meantime, he lives in Warwick with his wife and children. He writes in a tiny room, not much bigger than a wardrobe, which is crammed with books, pieces of paper and empty chocolate bar wrappers. His hobbies include fixing old computers and wishing he had more hobbies.

www.simoncheshire.co.uk